Thumbprint Mysteries

CHAMPAGNE AT THE MURDER

BY

JOAN LOWERY NIXON
AND
KATHLEEN NIXON BRUSH

CONTEMPORARY BOOKS
a division of NTC/CONTEMPORARY PUBLISHING GROUP
Lincolnwood, Illinois USA

Thumbprint
Mysteries

ABT-8437

MORE THUMBPRINT MYSTERIES

by Joan Lowery Nixon
and Kathleen Nixon Brush:

Champagne at Risk
Champagne with a Corpse

This is a work of fiction. The characters, incidents, and dialogues are products of the author's imagination and are not to be construed as real. Any resemblance to actual events or persons, living or dead, is entirely coincidental.

Cover Design: Tom Spransey

ISBN: 0-8092-0670-6

Published by Contemporary Books,
a division of NTC/Contemporary Publishing Group, Inc.,
4255 West Touhy Avenue,
Lincolnwood (Chicago), Illinois 60646-1975 U.S.A.
Manufactured in the United States of America.

890 QB 0987654321

CHAPTER 1

The telephone recording worried me. "Sorry I missed you, Stacy," I heard my grandmother say. "I thought I could catch you at home since it's Saturday morning."

She was quiet for a moment. When she went on, her voice shook a little. "I really need to talk to you about a problem that has come up," she said. "You always have such good ideas. And you've always been able to stay calm, no matter what. So when dreadful things happen . . ."

Again there was silence before Gran said, "I shouldn't have called. I didn't mean to bother you with a problem that isn't your concern. Just forget I called, darling."

The machine beeped once. Then a friend's voice came on. Chris was inviting me to lunch, but I only half-listened. My mind was on my grandmother. A problem had come up that must have frightened her. She needed me.

I dialed the telephone number of our family's hotel in Silver Ridge. Silver Ridge is a beautiful town high in the Colorado mountains. It's a place that I love.

Dad answered the phone. As usual, his voice was cool and formal.

I didn't even take time to say hello. "This is Stacy, Dad," I said. "What's wrong?"

Dad waited a moment before he answered. "Nothing's wrong, Stacy," Dad said.

"There must be. Gran called while I was out. She said there was some kind of a problem. Let me talk to Gran."

"Your grandmother isn't here right now," Dad told me. "I'll tell her later that you called."

I wanted to shout, "Why can't you unbend for just a moment? I'm your daughter, not a hotel guest. You don't have to put on that stiff-necked dignity for me. And I'm not a child. You don't have to try to keep family problems from me."

I made myself calm down. "Dad," I said, "Gran told me there was a problem. Do you or Gran or Uncle Jim have some kind of a health problem?"

"Of course not," Dad said. "We are all in fine health."

"Then is there a problem with the hotel?"

"There are no problems," Dad said.

He put me on hold for a few seconds. Then he said, "Stacy, I'm busy with a group of hotel guests who are checking in right now. Please forget about your grandmother's telephone call. She had no right to break into your life and cause you worry."

"But, Dad, I need to know." I lowered my voice. "Let me talk to Uncle Jim."

"Not now. I don't know where Jim is," Dad said.

"Dad!"

"Sorry, dear. I *am* very busy."

I felt hurt and lonely and homesick. I sighed and said, "Okay, Dad. Good-bye. I love you."

All I got was a dial tone. *Couldn't you say, "I love you, too?"* I thought. *I don't care if a hotel guest is staring at you across the desk, waiting for a room key!* I slammed down the phone.

Something was wrong enough to worry Gran. So why didn't my father want to tell me what it was?

I took a deep breath. Then I dialed my assistant's office number at Talented Temps. That's where I work as branch manager of the Denver office.

"Hi, Adele. This is Stacy Champagne," I said into the telephone. "It's Saturday, around two o'clock. I'm going to drive to Silver Ridge. I should be back tomorrow and in the office on Monday. But if I'm not, please take over for me for a few days. Okay?" I left the number of our family hotel in Silver Ridge where Adele could reach me.

After I had gotten my degree from the University of Colorado, I'd expected to work in our family's hotel. But Dad had said, "Will you be job hunting in Colorado, Stacy? Or do you want to try another part of the United States?"

I'd gasped with surprise. "I thought you'd need me here," I said. "The Silver Ridge is our family hotel."

I hadn't had a chance to tell Dad that the Silver Ridge was *my* hotel too. I loved it, and I'd do a good job working at anything Dad wanted me to do.

Dad's voice had been firm. "You've lived in Silver Ridge all your life, Stacy. Now it's time for you to try your wings."

That's not what I'd wanted to hear. I'd wanted to be told I had a job in our family's hotel. I'd wanted to be told that if I left I'd be missed.

Maybe things would have been different if my mother hadn't died when I was four. Or maybe if my father weren't such a formal person. Or maybe if he and I had been closer while I was growing up. I sighed. "Maybes" didn't count. I wasn't wanted. That was clear. So there was no way I'd beg Dad for a job.

I was hired by Talented Temps in Denver. As I left Silver Ridge, Gran's eyes had filled with tears. Uncle Jim had looked like he did when his favorite dog died. But neither Gran, Uncle Jim, or Dad had said, "Please stay and work here, Stacy. We want you."

Over the next six years I'd gone home to visit. At first my visits came often. Then they grew farther apart. I'd been busy with my job and with new friends in Denver. It became harder to find time for visits home.

Gran's phone message had shaken me. All I knew was there was a problem that had frightened her. Gran hadn't talked about it. Dad wouldn't talk about it. But I had to know what it was. If I could help, I would. As I threw things into a suitcase, I felt a scared, tight ache in the pit of my stomach.

Two hours later I reached a favorite spot on the road to Silver Ridge. I slowed the speed of the car and swung to an overlook on the right side. A break in the forest framed a view across the valley to Silver Ridge.

I held my breath. I was afraid to break the silent beauty. The light spring leaves of aspen shone against the background of dark pine, alpine fir, and silvery blue spruce. On a rise, overlooking the town, sat the beautiful Silver Ridge Hotel.

It was built of dark red brick with wood trim. A round stone tower with a pointed roof rose at the right-hand side. A narrow, wood-trimmed balcony spread across the second story. The most recent paint job had turned the woodwork into soft shades of beige and blue. The look was warm and welcoming.

Three generations of Champagnes had run this hotel since my great-grandfather had emigrated to the United States. And I had grown up in it. I had roller-skated on the veranda. I'd played dolls behind the big sofas in the lobby. I'd gone to school dances in the ballroom. And I'd learned the hotel business from my grandparents, my father, and my Uncle Jim.

I was still homesick—not only for my family, but for the hotel. I loved its creaky elevators, high-ceilinged rooms, and long, quiet hallways. I smiled as I thought of its busy kitchen. I couldn't count the many times I'd been given a secret snack of cake or cookies by the chefs.

I put the car back into drive. I headed down the road toward Silver Ridge.

When I arrived at the hotel, I found a space in the parking lot at the west side. I left my luggage in the car and entered an outside door in the right wing. I was sure Dad would be behind the front desk. I didn't want to see him until I'd talked to Gran. The trick now would be to find Gran.

As I neared the main lobby, a door opened. A big hand shot out, grabbed my arm, and pulled me into the office of the Chief of Security.

Uncle Jim grinned down at me. Then he wrapped me in a hug. "Stacy! I'm so glad to see you!" he said.

As he backed off he looked puzzled. "Is this a holiday?" he asked. "Is that why you're here?"

"I'm here because Gran called," I said. "I got her message. She said there was a problem. Tell me. What *is* the problem?"

Uncle Jim thought hard for a few minutes. I waited until he was ready. There was no hurrying Uncle Jim.

A poet once wrote about the West, "Give me men to match my mountains." Nature had answered with Uncle Jim. He was six feet, six inches tall, strong, and broad-shouldered.

I think he was given the job of the Silver Ridge Hotel's Chief of Security only because of his size. It wasn't because he liked the job. As a matter of fact, he didn't like it at all. Uncle Jim was an outdoors man. He hated working at a desk. But he had a strong sense of family. Gran gave him this job because she felt he was suited to it. So Jim did whatever was needed, even though he longed to be outside hunting or fishing.

At last Uncle Jim raised his head and looked at me with sad eyes. "Your grandmother has allowed Will Knight to stay here while he destroys this town."

"Destroys the town?" I cried. "That makes no sense. Who is Will Knight? What's this all about?"

Uncle Jim picked up a newspaper from his desk. He opened it to the editorial page. "It will make sense when you read this," he said. "Barry wrote an editorial about it in the paper. He wrote a front-page story, too, about the threat to Silver Ridge."

Some things never change. Barry Harrison, our town's only local printer, had been editor of the weekly newspaper, *The Silver Ridge Times*, ever since I could remember. His newspaper came out every Tuesday morning without fail. *The Times* gave its readers the local news they wanted. Most of it had to do with church suppers or high school football scores. It was hard to think of Barry writing anything more serious.

I reached for the paper, but the door opened. Uncle Jim stepped back, out of the way. "Excuse me, sir," said the man in the doorway.

He was wearing the tan uniform of a deputy sheriff. With his dark hair, trim mustache, and deep brown eyes, he looked as if he'd stepped out of an old photograph: "Lawman of the Old West." He was handsome and tall—just a couple of inches shorter than my uncle.

"Mr. James Champagne, I'm Deputy Ramon Gonzales," the deputy said. He shook hands with Uncle Jim. Then he glanced in my direction and smiled. A terrific smile.

"This is my niece, Stacy Champagne," Uncle Jim said.

Ramon smiled again, but he turned back to Uncle Jim. "The sheriff has assigned me to help out here," he said. "We've heard that there may be a protest march at your hotel on Monday."

"What protest? What's it about?" I asked.

The door flew open, and my grandmother, Lydia Champagne, stood in the doorway. As usual, Gran looked great. She's slender and trim, with beautiful high cheekbones—a bonus from her own grandmother, a Native American from the Lakota people.

"Gran!" I called. I ran to hug her.

Her face lit up with happiness. "Stacy, my little love! You're here! This is wonderful!"

"You told me there was a problem," I said. I suddenly remembered my manners and introduced Ramon. Then I asked Gran, "What's going on?"

Gran looked surprised. "Didn't Jim tell you about Will Knight?"

I took a deep breath. I'd have to be patient and try to get the information one step at a time. "First tell me, who is Will Knight?"

"Will grew up here in Silver Ridge," Gran said. "He was in Jim's class in high school. During his senior year, he and his family moved somewhere on the East Coast. That's the last we would have heard of Will, I guess, except that he married a local girl—Juliana Martin. Now, Will and Juliana are coming here to stay a few days at our hotel."

Uncle Jim gave a low growl, and his face turned red. I remembered hearing about the beautiful Juliana. She had been Uncle Jim's first love. "You didn't have to accept their reservation," he said.

"Of course I did," Gran told him. "It would have been rude to turn them away."

I quickly asked another question. "Is Will Knight coming back to see old friends?"

"Oh, no," Gran said. "Around Silver Ridge Will hasn't got any friends." Her forehead wrinkled, and I could see real worry in her eyes. She sighed as she said, "I'm afraid Will Knight is coming back to reopen the silver mine."

CHAPTER 2

Deputy Gonzales began questioning Uncle Jim, so I put an arm around Gran's waist and led her through the lobby.

Two years ago I had helped cover the matched pair of sofas in a soft, blue fabric. I was glad to see that they still looked beautiful. The whole lobby looked wonderful with new, deep-gold carpet and blue-striped chairs. At the far left side of the room was the original reception desk. Its highly polished wood gleamed.

I waited until we were seated in Gran's office. Then I asked, "Do you think that opening the silver mine will be a threat to the hotel? Is that why you're worried?"

"It's a threat to the entire town," she answered. "I don't understand Will Knight's thinking."

"Or his wife Juliana's thinking," I said.

Gran spoke up quickly. "Oh, I don't blame Juliana. She was such a sweet girl." She slowly shook her head. "I

9

can't imagine why she married Will, though. He always was a troublemaker."

"Did he grow up here in Silver Ridge?" I asked.

"Will and his parents moved here when he was in his last year of high school," she said. "He graduated, but he was always in trouble. After graduation he went to work for his father. But he still kept getting into trouble."

"What kind of trouble?"

"There was a group of high school seniors just a year or two younger than Will. They were nice kids at heart, but with Will around they seemed to go a little wild."

"Was Uncle Jim one of them?" I asked.

"No, thank goodness," Gran said. "And Juliana wasn't either. At least, I thought she wasn't. But then she suddenly married Knight, and no one could understand it."

"Especially Uncle Jim?"

Gran sighed. "Well, what's over is over. They moved away, and so did Will's parents. Jim went on to fall in love with someone else . . . and someone else . . . and someone else."

There was a knock on the door, and the deputy poked his head into the office.

"Excuse me, ma'am," he said to Gran. "You might want to know that a car just came up the drive. Mr. Champagne said the Knights are here."

"Thank you," Gran said. She stood and led Ramon and me into the lobby.

We halted at the edge of the main desk. I quickly glanced over my shoulder and saw that the door to the security chief's office stood partly open. I wondered if Uncle Jim was waiting there to see his first love walk into view.

There were two desk clerks behind the reception counter—Gloria and Keshia. They recognized me and smiled. Gloria gave me a wink before she turned back to the guest she was helping.

Dad's back was to us as he spoke on the phone. But the moment he hung up Gran said, "Charles, look who's come home!"

Dad quickly turned. There was the familiar look he got on his face when he was greeting hotel guests. But as he saw me his eyes softened. He came out from behind the desk. "Stacy, my dear," he said, "we weren't expecting you."

I wished Dad would hold out his arms in a hug, but he didn't. I knew he didn't like to show his feelings in public, but after all, we hadn't seen each other since Christmas. Well, if that was the way he wanted it, then okay. I wouldn't hug him either.

Suddenly, the Knights walked through the front door, and we all turned to look. Dad stepped forward with his right hand out to welcome our visitors.

Will Knight was tall, and his dark hair was stylish. He came into the room talking into a cell phone. He didn't even look at Dad. I've met people like Will Knight before. They think hotel people exist only to follow their orders.

On the other hand, Dad has always been interested in people. He likes to personally greet the hotel's guests. He also keeps notes about his guests' special likes and dislikes, their families, their interests, their allergies, and even their favorite foods. I could easily name half a dozen clients who stay each year at our hotel, instead of at some of the more elegant Colorado resort hotels, just because they like the way they're treated by Charles Champagne.

Obviously Will Knight wasn't one of them. But just as Dad let his arm drop, Juliana Knight quickly moved forward and shook his hand.

I could see why Uncle Jim had fallen in love with Juliana. She must not have changed much since high school. Her blond hair fell in smooth waves to her shoulders. Her eyes were warm as she smiled.

Dad began making introductions. Juliana turned to me and said, "You look so much like your lovely mother." Juliana won my instant friendship. I rarely met anyone who spoke to me about my mother.

"I know there must be people and places you'd like to revisit," Dad said to Juliana. "I'll be glad to help you locate any of your friends who still live in Silver Ridge."

Juliana frowned. She looked like a worried child. "I don't want you to go to any trouble, Mr. Champagne. I just—"

"Barry Harrison is coming," Gran said. She used the same dread tone of voice she used when reading weather reports about blizzards on the way.

Dad calmly said, "Barry owns our local newspaper now, Mrs. Knight. You remember him, don't you? I believe he was in your class in high school."

"Before I meet anyone," Juliana said quickly, "I'd like to check in and go to my room." She tugged at her husband's arm, pulling him forward. Will came without question, still intent on his phone call.

Everyone snapped into action. Dad handed a room key to one of our bellmen, Lew Parker. Lew was standing nearby with the Knights' suitcases on a cart. "Mr. Knight's suite," Dad said.

At the same time, Gran marched toward the hotel's entrance to block Barry's progress.

Dad handed me a second room key. "Why don't you take Mrs. Knight to her room?" he asked. So I followed the Knights and Lew into the elevator.

Lew punched the button for the fourth floor. But before

the doors closed I saw Jack O'Connor walk out of the coffee shop. Jack, who is my uncle's age, owns a clothing store in Silver Ridge. Jack had gone to school with Uncle Jim, Will, and Juliana. Jack is short and plump with wispy hair and a round, baby face. He usually has a happy-go-lucky manner. But now he stared at the Knights until the elevator doors closed. The look of hatred on his face made me shudder.

Will hadn't noticed. He was busy shouting, "Hello! Hello! We have a bad connection!" into the phone. But Juliana had seen Jack O'Connor. Her face was so pale it scared me.

We reached the fourth floor where our largest, most elegant suites were located. Lew and Will went toward a door just a short distance from the elevators. I led Juliana down the hall in the opposite direction.

"Lew will bring your bags to your room in just a few minutes," I said.

When he did, I placed them on our hotel's folding luggage racks. Lew checked the room's temperature, raised one of the windows a crack, and turned on our local radio station. He thanked Juliana for the generous tip and left me with the luggage trolley.

"Is there anything else I can do for you?" I asked Juliana.

She still seemed ill at ease. "No, thank you," she said. Then she suddenly blurted out, "I suppose you think it's odd that with my husband having a whole suite, I wanted a separate room. You see, Mr. Knight will be having business meetings in his suite. Everyone will be very busy."

"Of course," I said. I wondered why she was so eager to explain.

She looked at the cases and said, "Oh, dear! That small one shouldn't be here. It belongs to my husband."

I picked it up and said, "I'll take it to him."

"You're thoughtful, too, like your mother was."

Business was business. But talking to Juliana about my mother seemed much more important. "Tell me about her," I begged.

"Laura was tall and very pretty," Juliana said. "You even walk the way she did, with long steps and your shoulders back. And she had a wonderful sense of humor. Laura could see the funny side of almost every problem. Are you like that, Stacy?"

"Not always," I said. "Although there are quite a few times when I do my best to go ha-ha instead of oh-no."

Juliana laughed. "I knew it. You do have a good sense of humor."

She told me a story I hadn't heard about the time my mom entered a contest and tried to write an inspiring song about Silver Ridge. Juliana sang what she remembered of it, and we both began to laugh.

However, my sense of duty was stronger than the happy glow inside me. It was time to get back to business. "Thank you," I said.

I could see why Uncle Jim had loved Juliana. I was filled with fond thoughts about her too. I handed her the room key and left, quietly closing the door.

As I walked to Will Knight's room, I saw a piece of paper lying just outside his door. I picked it up. I'd been trained in neatness ever since I could toddle around with my toy broom after the head housekeeper.

The paper was a sheet of plain white paper, folded in half. I opened it to see if it was important or could be tossed. My fingers began to shake as I read, *Remember, Will Knight, Silver Ridge will be your death.*

CHAPTER 3

I wasn't sure what to do with this threatening letter. I didn't want to give it to Will Knight so I put it into my sweater pocket. Then I knocked on Will's door.

The door jerked open. He was still on the phone. I held out the case. He took it and closed the door. I walked across to the elevator.

A small man with thin, pale hair hopped off the elevator as the doors opened. He took one look at the luggage cart and said, "You work here. You'd know. Is this hotel haunted?"

"Of course not, Mr. . . . Mr. . . ."

"Thomas Laird," he said. "I *did* see a ghost."

Every once in a while we have a guest who thinks because our hotel is so old we should have a ghost in it. Why a mountain man, a miner, or a dance hall girl would want to haunt the Silver Ridge Hotel, I have no idea.

However, here was the first guest who said he'd really seen a ghost.

"The ghost was female. She was dressed in black. And she was on this floor, at the far end of the hall," Mr. Laird said. "I closed my eyes for a moment. When I opened them to take another look, the ghost had gone."

I didn't know what to tell Mr. Laird. So I said, "Find my uncle, Jim Champagne. He's Chief of Security. You can tell him about the ghost."

I hurried into the elevator and rode alone to the lobby. I was surprised when I stepped out of the elevator. Barry Harrison was blocked from the elevators by my grandmother and my uncle. The new deputy stood in back of my family. He watched Barry carefully.

"All I want is an interview," Barry said. "Why are you taking Knight's side?" He turned to me. "Stacy, you're here to fight the opening of the mine, aren't you?"

I didn't know why they were arguing, so I said, "I'm here to help my family."

"What's the matter with you people?" Barry was angry.

"We can't be rude to our guests," Gran said. "And we can't let you be rude to them either. We're working in our own way to help Silver Ridge."

Barry shook his head. "I seem to be the only one in Silver Ridge who cares what happens."

"That's where you're wrong," Gran told him. "I heard that Millie is working to have the mine named as a historical area. That will stop Will!"

"That would take forever," Barry grumbled. He turned and left the hotel.

Gran turned to Ramon. "Will you join us for our family dinner?" she asked.

"Thanks. I'd like to," Ramon said. He smiled at me.

We went upstairs to the second floor and sat around the table in our small kitchen. Gran handed around steaming bowls of potato soup that our wonderful chef, Eddie Jackson, had sent up from the kitchen. As we ate, Uncle Jim read aloud the headline on the front page of *The Times*: KNIGHT PLOTS TO DESTROY SILVER RIDGE.

"Barry must hate Will Knight," I said.

"He has ever since they were high school seniors," Dad told me. "Barry was hoping for a full scholarship to the university. He probably would have got it. But Will got Barry into a fight on the school grounds. They were both suspended from school for three days. Will got what he wanted. Barry lost his chance for the scholarship."

"Barry wasn't alone in hating Will," Jim said. "We all did. We all *do*."

"Can I ask a question?" Ramon asked Gran. "Why are you all so upset about having the silver mine reopened?"

"To reopen the mine would mean using a great deal of water. There wouldn't be enough water for both the mining and tourists who visit here. The town depends upon tourists."

"Also, the heavy metals from the mine would pollute the water we do have," Uncle Jim added.

"In that case, we should be able to stop Will Knight legally," I said.

"I can think of an easier way to stop him," Uncle Jim said. He made a noise through his teeth as he drew the side of his hand across his throat.

"Jim! Don't talk like that!" Gran said. She turned to me. "Stacy, will you please talk to Millie? Help her get that historical protection plan started."

The next morning I set off to visit Millie Blair at the historical museum where she works. I passed the coffee shop and saw Uncle Jim with Juliana. They were having coffee together. Poor Uncle Jim looked as lovesick as I had ever seen him.

As I came down the outside steps of the hotel I met Ramon. He wasn't wearing his uniform. He was dressed in a wool plaid shirt and jeans.

"Aren't you being a sheriff today?" I asked.

"Today's my day off," Ramon said. "I thought I'd better learn more about the people in Silver Ridge.

"You've already been to the hotel. You know about us."

"Not enough," he said quietly. I liked the smile that went with the words. "Where are you going, Stacy? Mind if I come along?"

We walked down Main Street to the museum, a two-story, red brick building set back from the busy street by a courtyard. At the door I signed the book as a museum member. My family had been members ever since Donald Blair had first begun the museum. A few years ago Mr. Blair retired to Denver. Now Millie, who had always worked at the museum, was in charge.

We were the only ones in the museum. We walked through the rooms with their displays of Native Americans, mountain men, and silver miners. On every display were printed cards. Millie had printed them herself on an old printing press that had been given to the museum. I didn't stop to read them. I'd read them years ago.

Millie came into the room we were in. She was small and thin, and she wore an old-fashioned, long, black dress. "Stacy! It's you!" she said. "What are you doing in Silver Ridge?"

I quickly introduced Ramon. Then I talked about how opening the silver mine would hurt our town.

Millie didn't meet my eyes. "There isn't much we can do," she said.

"Yes there is," I told her. "We can get angry. We can join the march at the hotel. We can write letters."

Millie didn't say anything. So I asked, "Aren't you going to try to get the Colorado Historical Society to name the mine a historical monument so it can't be opened and mined?"

Millie shook her head. "That was one of your grandmother's ideas. It wasn't mine. Besides, Will isn't the kind of man who does what he's told."

"Oh, that's right," I said. "You knew him when he lived here, didn't you? Did you know him well?"

To my surprise I saw fear in Millie's eyes. She took a deep breath and said, "I didn't know him well, no matter what you've heard. Now please excuse me. I'm very busy."

I could see that she wasn't busy at all. Ramon and I were the only guests in the museum. Somehow I'd frightened Millie. And it had to do with what she knew about Will Knight.

Millie hurried away, so Ramon and I left the museum.

"Why was she wearing a costume?" Ramon asked me.

I said. "She almost always dresses like that, even when she's not working inside the museum. Millie loves the history of Silver Ridge."

"She's afraid of something," Ramon said. "Do you have any idea what it is?"

"It must have to do with Will Knight," I said. There were some questions I thought I'd better ask my grandmother.

We walked down the main street with its lovely old brick houses and trim wooden buildings. A breeze blew through the rows of trees planted along the street. Colorful spring bulbs bloomed in tubs and window boxes in front of each shop. "I love springtime in Silver Ridge," I said.

"Why did you leave Silver Ridge to live in Denver?" Ramon asked me.

His question surprised me. There was no way I was going to tell him that I left because my family didn't want me to stay.

"I have a job in Denver," I said. "I'll be going back."

"Back to heavy traffic and long hours?" Ramon asked. "Why? I gave up city life. You could too."

"People only come to the mountains when they have something to escape," I began. The look of pain on his face startled me.

"Maybe you're right. Maybe I am escaping," he said. "You may as well know my reason for coming to the mountains. When I was a police officer in Houston, my partner and I answered a call about a family argument. The husband was holding his wife with a gun at her head. We saved her, but my partner was shot. He died." Ramon stopped talking for a moment. I could see how much this hurt him. "I needed to move on," he said. "I chose a small town."

I put a hand on his arm. "Ramon, I'm sorry," I said.

He took my hand into one of his, where it fit very comfortably. "Someday," he said, "you'll have to tell me why you thought you'd have to escape *from* the mountains."

"Someday," I said. "Not now."

I looked up the hill at the Silver Ridge Hotel and got a lump in my throat. I loved the hotel. I loved the cool air. I loved the beauty of the mountains. I knew that whatever Millie Blair feared, she was wrong. The only thing to fear was losing our past, our dreams, and our vivid green mountains to a short-term mining operation.

CHAPTER 4

When I got to the hotel, there was a police car blocking the path of a white sports car. Will Knight sat in the sports car. He glared at Police Officer Drew Morgan. Officer Morgan, who was built like a football player, glared right back.

"Get your arm off my car!" Will shouted.

Officer Morgan was in charge, no doubt about it. He waited until Will's face had turned bright red. Then he said, "You can't drive in a way that threatens the lives of the citizens of Silver Ridge."

Will waved a slip of paper at Morgan. I'd received one of those once. So I knew it was a traffic ticket.

I couldn't hide, and I couldn't return to town. I tried to walk past the sports car. I pretended I hadn't heard or seen a thing.

But Will noticed me. "You! Girl!" he shouted as he got out of the car. "You're with the hotel. Here are my car keys. Park my car in the underground garage. Turn the keys in at the desk. I'll be waiting for them."

He threw the keys at me so hard they stung my hand. Slamming the door of the car, Will stomped into the hotel.

I hurried to start the car. I drove it into the underground garage and parked it.

I had one hand on the door to open it when I froze. From the corner of my eye I saw Juliana Knight creeping next to the wall of the garage.

Every few feet she stopped and looked around. I didn't want to frighten her, so I sat without moving until she left the garage by the door at the back.

I ran from the car and followed Juliana to the garden. Beyond the garden was a path that led into the woods. I saw Juliana run down the path. I was ready to follow when, to my surprise, I saw a man step out from the shelter of the trees. He and Juliana walked into the forest and out of my sight.

What had I just seen? The man Juliana had crept away to meet was not her husband, who was probably still waiting in the lobby for his car keys. And it wasn't my lovesick Uncle Jim. The man was Silver Ridge's best chef, Eddie Jackson!

I hurried upstairs to the lobby. I put the car keys into an envelope and wrote Will's name on it.

Dad stopped sorting the mail. He still had a few letters in his hand. "How did your meeting go with Millie Blair?" he asked.

I didn't answer. I gasped and grabbed the top envelope he was holding.

"Stacy, that isn't for you," Dad said.

"I recognize the print," I said. I turned the envelope over in my hand. There was no return address.

I reached into the pocket of my sweater for the letter I'd found on the floor outside Will's suite. I'd forgotten all about it. I pulled it out and handed it to Dad.

He read the letter and said, "I don't like this at all. Our guests shouldn't receive threatening letters while they're in our care."

"Look," I said. "The print on the letter and the envelope are the same."

"Where did you get this letter?" he asked.

I told him. "I didn't give Will Knight the letter I found, and we don't have to give him this one, either," I said.

"We have to give it to him," Dad said. "We can't tamper with the mail."

I frowned at the letter. Monday's date was on the postmark, so I could see it had been delivered a day late. "Dad," I said, "I know where else I've seen unusual printing like this. On the display cards in the museum."

Dad studied the letter and the envelope again.

"Believe me," I said. "I was just at the museum a short while ago. This print isn't as dark or as large as the printing on Millie's signs, but it's the same style. You can see that it comes from an old press. I don't think there are any others around like it."

I took the letter I'd found and put it back into my pocket. A strange feeling swept over me. "Look at the hotel's address on this letter," I said. "It doesn't say *Silver Ridge, Colorado*. It just says *City*. Dad, it was mailed here in town!"

Dad frowned. "Surely you don't think that Millie Blair had anything to do with this?"

But I did. I remembered the fear in Millie's eyes. No wonder she was afraid to openly fight Will Knight's plan if she'd been sending him threatening letters.

Just then Jane Wilson, Dad's secretary, came out of the office. Her eyes lit up when she saw me. "Stacy, we're a little short-handed. Can you help set up for a luncheon?"

She headed for one of our elegant, small dining rooms. I trotted after her.

"By the way," Jane said, "this morning I called a friend of mine who manages a restaurant in Houston. I just happened to tell her that our new deputy was from Houston."

"I only met him yesterday. You don't have to do a background check on him."

Jane opened her eyes wide. "Stacy, this has nothing to do with *you*!" she said. "I thought you'd want to know that Ramon Gonzales is a hero. The story was in the news for days. He saved a woman being held at gunpoint. Unfortunately, another policeman was killed."

"Don't mention it to him," I warned. "His partner was the one who was shot. It hurts Ramon to talk about it." It hurt me, too, just thinking about the pain he was still in.

"Oh, I understand," Jane said. She looked at me carefully. "It seems as though you know him better than we—I—thought."

We arrived at the dining room. I opened the door and saw that everything was in place. Jane hadn't needed me. She'd just wanted to talk about Ramon. Since there was nothing I could do in the dining room, I headed for the coffee shop. I badly needed a cup of coffee.

Until later that afternoon I kept busy at a number of jobs. Then around four-thirty or so, I ran into Uncle Jim at the elevators. He was carrying a large basket of fruit on a tray. With it was a pair of napkins, two china plates, and one of our hotel's beautiful silver fruit knives. We give these trays to special guests.

I looked at the card and shook my head. "I don't think Will Knight rates a fruit basket."

"This isn't my idea," Jim grumbled. "It's your grandmother's. This is the second tray I've brought to Knight. He didn't like the selection of fruit on the first tray. 'No kiwis or figs,' he said. 'I only like oranges and apples.'" Uncle Jim scowled as he stepped into the elevators and the door closed.

Two hours later I was with Gran, eating a quick supper. The telephone rang, and she answered it. As she hung up, she said, "That was Nadine. Will asked to have the sitting room of his suite set up for a business meeting he's having in the morning. He wants it done while he's at dinner. He made reservations in *Champagne's* for an early six o'clock dinner."

I looked at my watch. "It's already six-thirty."

"I know," Gran said. "And Nadine has her hands full. She asked if you'd help out."

"I'll be glad to," I said. I got to my feet.

At exactly six thirty-seven I knocked at the door of Will Knight's suite. I didn't get an answer, so I opened the door with my passkey. I backed into the room, pulling a cart with extra folding chairs balanced on it.

The room was nearly dark since the sun had already made its rapid drop behind the mountain peaks. I reached for the light switch and flooded the sitting room of the suite with brightness.

It was then that I saw the body.

CHAPTER 5

Will Knight was lying face down on the floor with one hand outstretched. He seemed to be reaching out to me.

I took a slow, deep breath. "Mr. Knight?" I whispered.

He didn't move.

In panic I bent down and rolled him over onto his back.

No question about it, Will Knight was very cold and very dead. A silver fruit knife from the Silver Ridge Hotel protruded from a bloody gash in his chest.

I stood up shakily and staggered out of the room. I locked the door to the suite behind me and used my passkey to enter an empty room down the hall. I suppose I should have called the front desk, but for some reason I called Gran.

"Gran!" I said. "Will Knight has been murdered. Get hold of Uncle Jim. Tell him to call the police." I thought about Will's bloody shirt and shivered. "Don't let Juliana come up here."

I hung up, afraid to leave the room until I heard the ping of the elevator.

First out of the elevator was Officer Morgan. With him were two uniformed policemen, Ramon, my father, and Dr. Tower, our local doctor. I wondered where Uncle Jim was. Maybe Gran had asked him to find Juliana.

Ramon came forward and grabbed my shoulders. "Are you all right?" he asked.

I nodded. I felt much better with Ramon standing by.

"What's going on, Stacy?" Officer Morgan asked me.

I pointed toward the door to Will's room. "In there," was all I could say.

"Okay. You wait here," Morgan said to me.

Dad opened the door with his passkey, and the group quickly went inside. But Dad waited. He looked at me with worry. "Are you sure you're all right?" he asked.

"Yes," I said, "but *you* don't look well, Dad." I led him to one of the small chairs that were grouped across from the elevators. I sat next to him. We didn't talk. We just waited.

Finally Morgan and Ramon came out of Will's room together. "I'll handle this," Morgan said. "You tell your sheriff to find his own murder."

"We're supposed to be on the same side. Don't fight me on this," Ramon said.

They looked up and saw us watching them.

"What are you doing there?" Morgan growled.

"You told me to wait for you," I said.

Morgan leaned against the wall. "Stacy," he said, "I need to know exactly what happened."

I told him and answered his questions. Just then the doctor came out of Will's room. "I'll write up a report for you, and you'll get a coroner's report from the county. But I can tell you the cause of death right now."

"We could all see the cause of death," Morgan snapped. "He was stabbed in the heart with a fruit knife. I need to know other things. Like, what was the time of death?"

Doctor Tower thought a moment. "The room's at a normal temperature. I'd say he died sometime between about five and six, give or take half an hour each way. Now, are you ready to tell his wife?"

Ramon said, "Wait. I've got something to show you." He reached into his pocket and took out a plastic bag. From the bag he took an envelope and sheet of paper.

I knew what it was. It was the letter that had come for Will that afternoon.

"This was in Knight's waste basket," Ramon said. He read aloud, *"I read about your plan to open the mine. You won't get away with destroying this town. Silver Ridge will be your death."*

Morgan stared at the envelope. He said, "That print looks kind of familiar."

"You know what it reminds me of?" Dr. Tower said. "The printing on the posters and cards in Millie's museum."

"But it's a lot smaller than the printing on the signs in the museum," I said.

"There are ways to reduce print size," Ramon answered. "Maybe we should talk to Millie about this."

"We're going to talk to a lot of people," Morgan snapped. "Downstairs, everyone."

The five of us rode down in silence on the elevator. I don't know how the others felt, but I was frightened. I realized I was holding in my sweater pocket what might turn out to be important evidence. A *second* threatening letter!

Gran met us in the lobby. She looked a little pale, but she was still in charge. "Juliana is waiting for you in my office," she said to Morgan. "I haven't told her yet, but I'll be glad to go with you while you do."

"Thanks. I wish you would," Morgan answered.

I took Ramon aside. "I need to tell you something important." I led him to a sofa at the far wall and sat next to him. I pulled the sheet of paper from my pocket and handed it to him. Then I told him how I'd found it.

"This looks like the same printing," he said. "Look at that curl on the letter *p*. See how the *e* is slightly closed. What do you think, Stacy? Did this come from the museum press? Who has access to it? How often is it used?"

I sighed. "I don't know," I said and pointed toward the crowd that was beginning to gather in the lobby. "Why don't you ask Millie? She's over there with her brother, Jack."

As Ramon and I stood up, Morgan came out of Gran's office. Behind him came Juliana, who was leaning against my Uncle Jim. Following them were Gran and Dad. Morgan left the others at the elevator. He motioned to Ramon and me to join him.

Before we reached him, Morgan pulled Jack and Millie out of the crowd. "I have some questions you can answer for me," he said. He turned to me. "Stacy, find us a quiet place to talk."

I led them to the Napoleon room.

"Everybody sit down," Morgan ordered. "I want to get some information about what happened tonight."

Ramon looked at Morgan with surprise. "Don't you want to question each person separately?"

"Do I have to tell you again, this is *my* case?" Morgan answered. He pulled out a plastic bag which held the printed letter. "This letter makes me wonder—"

The door opened. Barry Harrison stuck his head into the room. "Officer Morgan, I need some information from you for a news story," he said.

"Get in here, Barry, and sit down," Morgan said. "You know about printing, so you can help out on this."

Barry picked up the nearest chair. He flipped it around and sat astride it.

"Now," Morgan said. He held out the letter. "Take a look at the printing. Isn't it a lot like the printing you do in the museum, Jack?"

Millie gasped. "We don't have type that small."

"What about you, Barry?" Morgan asked.

Barry shook his head. "No. Anyone can see that's outdated. I couldn't get my machines to turn out anything like that."

Morgan frowned a moment. Then he said to Jack, "We found one of those little cigar-like things stubbed out in an ashtray in Knight's room. You're the only one I know who smokes them. What time today did you visit Knight?"

"Jack wouldn't hurt a fly!" Millie shouted.

"You don't have to defend me," Jack said. "I was with Knight about a quarter past three. I thought we could have a friendly chat about how he was going to ruin the town. About how people who'd lived here all their lives would have to move away."

"A friendly chat? Did you get through to him?"

Jack shook his head.

"Do you know how to operate that antique press in your sister's museum?"

"No, he doesn't!" Millie said.

Morgan turned to Barry. "What about you, Mr. Harrison? You were trying to get an interview with Knight. Did you finally get to see him?"

"I interviewed him at three this afternoon," Barry said.

"That must have been a very short interview if Jack saw him fifteen minutes later."

"I'm an efficient reporter."

"Did you talk about the threatening letter Knight had received?" Morgan asked.

"He showed me one that had just arrived. I didn't pay any attention to it. I was interested only in the information I needed for my news story."

Ramon surprised me with his question. "Did you talk over the lawsuit for libel Knight had filed against you and *The Silver Ridge Times?*"

Morgan frowned. "This is the first I've heard about any lawsuit," he said.

"A member of the sheriff's department delivered the papers to Barry Harrison this morning," Ramon told him.

Barry just smiled. "Sure. The lawsuit came up, but it wasn't important. Will and I talked about high school days. He even offered me something from his fruit basket, so we shared an apple. Then I asked him some questions about his plans for the old mine. Finally, I brought up the lawsuit. I knew that we could resolve it without going to court."

Millie jumped to her feet. "Come on, Barry! I heard you! You were both shouting!"

Morgan was surprised. "Were you there too, Millie?"

She looked embarrassed. "Well, I was in the hall. I couldn't help overhearing."

"Suppose you tell us what they were shouting about."

"I couldn't hear all of it," she said. "But I did hear Will laugh and say something about killing two birds with one stone. Then Barry yelled that he'd never get away with it. Then some guy in the suite to the left of Knight's suite opened his door. He gave me a funny look, so I left."

"What were you doing out in the hall in the first place?" Morgan asked.

"I was visiting Knight. I left his room just before Barry got there."

"Why did you go to see Knight?"

"And when?" Ramon asked.

"I don't know the exact time," Millie said unhappily. "But I went to see him because someone had to stop that terrible man. There was just one thing he'd understand."

She stopped, and we all just stared. Morgan's voice was slow and quiet. "Did you threaten him, Millie?"

"Of course, I threatened him," she said. "My family has lived in Silver Ridge since the beginning, and he wasn't about to make us move now."

Morgan held out the envelope. "So you sent him this letter?"

Millie waved the letter away. "Why should I waste time on a stupid letter he'd just throw in the trash?"

"Did you kill him?" Morgan's voice was gentle.

"Me?" Millie asked. "Of course not!"

Jack jumped up and put an arm around his sister. "Don't accuse Millie!" he shouted at Officer Morgan. "If you want to find out who killed Knight, why don't you talk to Jim Champagne?"

CHAPTER 6

"Don't try to blame my uncle!" I shouted at Jack. I wanted to say more about Uncle Jim's innocence, but I couldn't. I clearly remembered Uncle Jim taking that tray with the silver fruit knife up to Will Knight's room.

Jack ignored me. He said to Morgan, "Knight's door was open. I just happened to glance inside the room. I saw Jim trying to choke Knight."

"Didn't you try to stop him?"

Jack looked away. His face turned red. "Jim's a big guy," he said. "And Knight seemed to be holding his own."

"When was this?" Morgan asked.

"Sometime before four o'clock. I was looking for Millie. I wanted to walk home with her. I thought she might be talking over old times with Juliana."

"I was downstairs in the lobby waiting for you," Millie

broke in. "And you came down at exactly four o'clock, because I looked at my watch."

"When did Jim come downstairs?" Ramon asked.

No one answered. Finally, I said, "I don't like this talking behind his back. Why don't you just ask him?"

"Right," Morgan said. "I'd like to hear what Jim has to say." He turned to Ramon and said, "Come on."

Morgan strode out of the room. Ramon followed him. I followed Ramon. No one was going to railroad my uncle while I was around!

Uncle Jim came out of the Chief of Security's office just as we arrived. "Where have you been all evening?" Officer Morgan asked him. "Aren't you supposed to be in charge of security for the hotel?"

"Mom wanted me out from underfoot so I went fishing," Jim said.

"That's right," I said quickly. I knew that Gran wanted to keep Jim away from Juliana.

Ramon said to my uncle, "We know you saw Will Knight this afternoon. Jack O'Connor told us you were there. What time did you go up to Knight's room?"

"I don't know. What time did Jack tell you I was there?" Jim asked.

"Sometime before four," Morgan answered.

Ramon groaned. But Morgan didn't care about Ramon's opinion of his police work. "Why did you visit Knight?" Morgan asked Jim.

"To try to talk him out of opening the mine," Jim said.

Morgan closed in with another question. "When he wouldn't change his plans, you argued with him and maybe tried to choke him?"

"No. Why would I do that?" Jim looked puzzled.

"Jack told us you two were struggling," Morgan said.

"Oh, that." Jim shrugged. "Will got excited and swallowed the wrong way. I was just helping him catch his breath."

Morgan studied the notes he had made. "Okay. That should do it for now," he told Uncle Jim.

"What!" Ramon said. "That's all you're going to ask?"

Morgan didn't answer. He and Uncle Jim left the lobby. I asked Ramon, "Why didn't you tell Officer Morgan about the letter I found?"

"At this moment the letter is the property of the sheriff's department," Ramon said. "I'm going to send it to the crime lab to be tested."

Ramon walked me to the bottom of the stairs leading to our family's apartment. He would have come up, but I said, "Good night, Ramon. I'll see you tomorrow, I hope."

"Wouldn't you like a cup of coffee? Or a walk outdoors? I'd love to see the hotel grounds by moonlight."

"Not tonight," I said. "I'm really tired." I had to have time to get my thoughts together. I said good night and ran up the stairs into our apartment.

As I entered the living room, Gran looked up. "Stacy," she said, "I've already heard. Jim's a suspect." She sighed. "Morgan shouldn't have listened to Jack. For that matter, Morgan has questions to answer himself. This afternoon I saw Morgan come through the door from the stairs and go into Will's room."

I started. "When was this?"

"Around four-fifteen. I'd just brought Juliana some tea and muffins. I was leaving her room when I saw Officer Morgan going into Will's room. I'm afraid that Morgan is still bitter about what happened."

"What happened? I don't know."

"Oh, that's right. You wouldn't," she said. "It was when Will was still in high school. I told you what a troublemaker he was. Well, for a long time we all suspected Will of shoplifting. Arnold O'Connor—Millie and Jack's father—knew that Will had taken things from his store. He just hadn't caught him at it."

I remembered Arnold O'Connor. He rarely smiled. He could be awfully crabby to kids in his store. "What does this have to do with Morgan?" I asked.

"Arnold had seen Will stealing. He caught up with him in front of his store while someone called the police. Drew Morgan was the officer who answered the call. No one knows what happened, but when Will arrived at the police station he claimed that Officer Morgan had beaten him. Morgan said Will was lying. Will's parents threatened to sue."

"What did the investigation show?" I asked.

"Nothing was ever proved. The doctor in Silver Ridge agreed that Will was making things up. He couldn't find a mark on him. But Will's parents hired a specialist from Denver. He said the poor boy had back injuries."

Gran sighed. "The fuss finally died down, but Will's charges hurt Morgan's career. He might very well have become our police chief if there hadn't been that doubt about him."

I realized why Ramon had wanted to analyze that letter without Morgan knowing about it. "Gran," I asked, "do you think Drew Morgan might have murdered Will Knight?"

I could see the fear in her eyes. "He had as much reason to kill him as anyone else. What's going on here, Stacy? One of the suspects is investigating the murder!"

Suddenly, the fear changed to hope. "Stacy, you have all those skills in researching people that you use in your job. You could be like one of those private investigators and get all the background information we'd need about Will Knight. Then we could put our heads together and figure out who really murdered him."

"What about Uncle Jim?" I asked. "He's Security Chief for the hotel."

"Your uncle isn't happy with that job," Gran said. "He only wants to be outdoors where he can hunt and fish." She paused and went on, "If you can, help him."

I held my breath, waiting for her to continue. *Say it, Gran. Say, 'Stacy, we need you. We want you to come back.'*

But she didn't. I kissed Gran good night and went to bed.

In the morning I read the newspaper while I ate breakfast. Reading kept me from having to decide what I should do to try to solve the murder. Barry had written a feature story about Glenda Sutton, an elderly resident who was celebrating her eightieth birthday. Barry had written a warm, funny, delightful story about her. No doubt about it, he was a talented writer. I remembered the story he wrote a couple of years ago about our hotel. He described every detail and made its history sound interesting.

I looked at my watch. Now was the perfect time to catch Nadine in Housekeeping. I could begin my questions with Nadine.

But as I entered the lobby, Thomas Laird rushed up to me. "I saw the ghost again," he said. "It was yesterday afternoon. A good day for me to write, I thought." Mr. Laird rolled his eyes. "But there was too much noise in the suite next door. First there was a loud argument with some woman about a man she was meeting. Then the woman left and I heard two male voices. They were even louder."

"That's when the ghost appeared to you?" I asked.

"It wasn't quite like that," Mr. Laird said. "The argument grew so loud I thought the men might be out in the hall. I opened my door so I could give them a stern look." He shuddered. "I caught a quick glimpse of the ghost I had seen earlier—that woman in black. She slowly began to turn toward me! Well! I couldn't shut the door fast enough! I hope you'll do something about it."

"The ghost?"

Mr. Laird shook his head. "No. The noise in the suite next door. It interferes with my writing."

I tried to be the perfect host. "You won't have any more trouble, Mr. Laird," I said. "I promise."

As he hurried away, I realized that I had learned one thing. I knew the so-called ghost that Mr. Laird had seen was Millie Blair.

I went to Nadine's office. Nadine and her housekeeping employees were the first line in security. They would report anything unusual that they noticed. And Nadine made sure they noticed.

"There were a lot of Silver Ridge people here yesterday," Nadine told me. "Jack O'Connor brought door prizes for the luncheon. Lily Chan came with her teenaged violin students to entertain the luncheon guests. Millie Blair came in costume, and there were a lot of other women here for the luncheon."

"Was anyone from Housekeeping on the fourth floor in mid- or late afternoon?"

Nadine shook her head. "No one in my department would have had any business being on the fourth floor at that time of day. But check with Eddie. Mr. Knight wanted to talk to him about the menu for his mine investors' banquet on Friday. Eddie went to his suite to talk to him."

"Do you know what time Eddie was there?"

"No," Nadine said. "Ask Eddie."

In the kitchen Eddie was marinating chicken breasts in a wonderful sauce that smelled of honey and spice. I learned when I was very young that the kitchen belongs to the chef. No one comes in without the chef's okay. So I called, "May I have permission to enter the kitchen?"

Eddie smiled. "Sure, Stacy. Want a taste of the chocolate bread pudding? It's the special tonight."

"Later," I said. "I want to ask you what happened when you met with Will Knight yesterday afternoon."

Eddie put down his basting spoon. "I didn't even see him. I went to the fourth floor. But before I could knock at Mr. Knight's door, I could hear him shouting at his wife."

"How do you know who he was shouting at?" I asked.

"He was shouting her name. I left, but I went back later. Barry had just come out of Mr. Knight's room. He told me that Mr. Knight was too upset to talk to anybody, so I didn't waste my time. I took the elevator back downstairs with Barry."

"Do you know the exact times you were there?"

Eddie thought a minute. Then he said, "After lunch and before dinner."

"That doesn't tell me what I need to know," I said.

Eddie smiled. "Funny. That's just what that deputy sheriff said."

CHAPTER 7

Barry's trenchcoat hung on an old wooden coatrack in a corner of the office of *The Times*. A press was spitting out some golden sheets of paper while Barry fed pink sheets to another machine. It shot them out neatly folded.

I didn't try to shout over the noise. I waited until Barry looked up and saw me.

He came over to the counter, and I asked, "You saw that threatening letter that was mailed to Mr. Knight, didn't you?"

"With the type that seems to have come from the old press at Millie's museum? Yes, I saw it." Barry shook his head. "I thought Millie would be more help."

"Millie and Jack did go to see Mr. Knight yesterday," I said. "Maybe they thought that as old friends they could change his mind."

"I'd hardly say they were old friends," Barry said.

40

"Millie did date Will a couple of times in high school. But Jack didn't like the guy. I wouldn't call that being old friends. In fact, I wouldn't put it past Millie to send Knight a threatening letter."

"Millie isn't the only one in town with a printing press," I said.

For a moment Barry looked angry. "You think I wrote the letter? You're as much of a suspect as anyone else. We'd all lose out if the mine was opened. But the loss of your hotel would be a huge problem for your entire family."

Just then the door opened, and Ramon came into the printing office. He gave me just one, quick look. Then he held out the plastic bag that held the threatening letter that had been mailed to Knight. "You can help me with this, Mr. Harrison. Can you tell me anything about the kind of printing that was used on this envelope?"

"Nothing more than I told the police last night," Barry said. "Now, if you and Morgan want to share information with me for my readers . . ."

Ramon put the envelope back into his pocket. "I do have a search warrant for the typeface that would have been used for this letter," he said. He handed the warrant to Barry.

Barry handed it back. "You won't find anything here."

"That's what I thought," Ramon said. "But I think you could tell me what I need to know to find out who printed this letter and how it was done."

Barry frowned. He said, "Excuse me, Stacy. I am required by law to show this deputy around my newspaper office."

Ramon didn't even look at me. So I left Barry's office, wondering why Ramon was acting so unfriendly. I walked up the street to O'Connor's store.

It was a pretty store with blue-and-white striped awnings over the windows. Red petunias bloomed in flowerpots on each side of the door. The store had just opened when I got there. Only one customer was searching through the dress racks.

Tess, Jack's plump, blond wife, came over to join Jack and me. She brought us cups of coffee.

"Tell me about your high school days with Will Knight," I said to Jack. "Were you friends?"

"Oh, yes. They were very good friends," Tess said.

"No, we weren't," Jack said. "We weren't even in the same class. I was younger. Besides, he hated me, and I hated him."

"Don't say that," Tess said. She looked worried. "I heard that you were his one good friend in Silver Ridge."

Jack sipped at his coffee. He hadn't seemed to get Tess's message. "Will was a showoff and a bully. He was a thief too."

"My grandmother told me that your father caught Will shoplifting," I said. "Was he arrested? Did he go to jail?"

"No," Jack said. "Morgan blew the arrest."

"Do you believe what Will said—that Morgan beat him?"

"I don't know. No one saw what happened. Will's parents threatened to sue both Morgan and Dad. Everyone hired lawyers. Finally, it all seemed to be over."

"Except for Drew Morgan," Tess said. "The charges really hurt his career. People were still talking about it when I moved to Silver Ridge." Her voice dropped. "It's just gossip, but I've heard that there were things Morgan wanted to hide."

"I guess just about everyone has something to hide," I said. "I wonder how many people think their secrets are hidden and don't realize that someone else knows."

I was thinking about Morgan, of course. But Jack's face turned red, and he breathed heavily. Tess's eyes were huge in her pale face. I was surprised. Did they think I meant them?

Tess hissed at me, "Be careful, Stacy. Sometimes knowing too much can be dangerous!" She hurried to help her customer.

Jack glared at me. I put down my empty cup and turned to leave. But the door opened and Ramon entered the store. I wished Ramon would smile at me. I wanted things to be friendly between us again. But he just gave me a quick nod and began to talk to Jack O'Connor. I left the store.

Juliana was in the lobby when I got back to the hotel. Gran was at her side.

As I joined them, Juliana said, "I'll see you later. I'm going for a walk."

"I'll get my sweater," Gran said.

I saw from the look on Juliana's face that Gran had been sticking close to her. She was making sure that Juliana and Uncle Jim couldn't have the chance to be alone. "You've been taking good care of Juliana," I said. "Now it's my turn."

"No one needs to go with me," Juliana began.

I interrupted. "I'd like a walk too. I'd like a chance to get to know you better."

There wasn't much Juliana could say to that. While Juliana went upstairs to get a sweater, Gran said, "Stacy, try to find out from Glenna Sutton what will happen to the old mine now that Will Knight is gone. She may know because she sold Will the property."

"I'll visit Glenna after I deliver Juliana back to the hotel," I promised.

Juliana came back with her sweater, and we began our walk to the main street of Silver Ridge. She kept insisting that I didn't need to come with her. I wondered why she was so eager to get rid of me.

She chatted about the beauty of the mountains, the flowers, and Silver Ridge. But she suddenly stopped and stared at a large poster in the window of our town's travel agency.

"I just thought of something," she said. "I haven't done a thing to change our reservations for our return flight to Florida. Wait right here, Stacy. I'll be back in a minute."

She darted through the door, closing it behind her. I didn't wait. I followed her inside.

Startled, Juliana said, "Stacy, will you please run out and get me some coffee?"

Mary Ann Broadhurst, who's been Silver Ridge's lone travel agent for ages, took off her glasses. She said, "There's a fresh pot on that table over in the corner. Help yourselves."

I poured Juliana a cup and added cream and sugar. By the time I came back to the desk, Juliana had given an envelope to Mary Ann.

Mary Ann pulled a lone airline ticket out of the envelope and studied it. I was close enough to see that it wasn't a ticket to Florida. It was Varig Airlines. I was sure that Varig flew out of Brazil.

"Hmmm. One way," Mary Ann said to herself.

Juliana looked up at me. I stared out the window as if I hadn't seen or heard a thing. *Why, Brazil?* I thought. Then I remembered that Brazil wouldn't send suspects back to the United States. Would that have been Juliana's reason for having bought a one-way ticket to Brazil? But if she wanted to murder her husband and leave the

Champagne at the Murder

country, she'd use the ticket. She wouldn't cash it in.

"No problem," Mary Ann said. "I'll take care of it for you."

Juliana stood and left the office. I hurried after her. She walked back toward the hotel. Tears came to her eyes as she said, "I've always loved Silver Ridge. I wish Will had understood that I couldn't have let him destroy this town."

I felt a cold chill run up my backbone. "You stopped him?" I whispered.

"I had to," she said.

"What are you telling me, Juliana?"

I could see her try to pull herself together. "It really doesn't matter now," she said. "What's done is done. It's for the best."

"Murder?" My voice came out in a croak.

Juliana smiled and put an arm around my shoulders. "I wasn't talking about murder," she said. "Come on. Let's get back to the hotel."

Uncle Jim was waiting when we walked into the lobby. But Gran was faster than he was. "I've ordered lunch to be sent to Juliana's room," she said. "She needs to rest."

She and Juliana disappeared before Uncle Jim could argue.

"Why are you all trying so hard to keep us apart?" Uncle Jim asked me.

"Because Juliana's a suspect. And you are too."

Uncle Jim scowled at me. "Are you suddenly in charge of security?"

I spoke before I thought. "You don't seem to be doing the job."

Uncle Jim got very quiet. "You're right, Stacy," he said softly.

I grabbed his arm. "Uncle Jim, I didn't mean to hurt you."

"No, it's time I faced up to it." There was real pain in his face as he said, "Maybe I've done it all for nothing."

"Done *what* for nothing?" I cried.

"I need to get out for a while," Uncle Jim said. He turned and squashed me in one of his bear hugs. Then he walked out the door.

As I stood there, Ramon came up to me. "Stacy," he said, "I'm sorry for the way I acted this morning. I thought you were trying to show me up. Later I heard that your grandmother had asked you to help investigate the murder."

"Who told you?" I asked.

"The whole town knows. They all have a lot of faith in you."

I had to smile.

"Could I follow in your footsteps?" Ramon asked. "I think that people have been opening up to you when they won't talk to me."

"I'm going to talk to Glenna Sutton. She sold the property to Mr. Knight," I told him. "It's about a twenty-minute drive out of town. Do you want to come with me?"

"Sure," Ramon said.

I should have been happy that the problem between us was over. But I couldn't get Uncle Jim off my mind. "Maybe I've done it all for nothing," he'd said. What had he done? What did he mean? Had Uncle Jim murdered Will Knight?

No! I wouldn't believe it. Not my Uncle Jim. I'd prove that my uncle was innocent. I'd prove it to everyone—even to myself.

Chapter 8

As I drove my car onto the highway, Ramon frowned. "Stacy, I'm worried about the investigating you're doing to please your grandmother," he said. "I wish you'd leave it up to us. Most hotels—"

I didn't let him finish. "The Silver Ridge Hotel is not just any hotel," I said. "It has been the heart of the town since the early Wild West mining-camp days. It has always been in our family."

"The murderer doesn't want to be known. He might try to stop you."

"I know that," I said. I wasn't as brave as I tried to seem. I'd known most of the suspects all my life. I was even related to one of them. I should be able to go to any one of them for help. But I couldn't. One of them was a murderer.

Ramon's voice cut into my thoughts. "Look! Over there!" he said.

I looked toward the spot where he was pointing. On the side of a hill was a herd of mountain sheep. Ramon grinned. "That's the kind of sight I came to the mountains for. It's beautiful here. It's still wild and free."

"You feel part of the mountains," I said.

Ramon sighed. "I may never be a part of these mountains. Right now, I'm both the new guy and the law. People are talking to you, Stacy, because you're one of them. But they're freezing me out. Since you insist on investigating, you could help me uncover the truth. What have you found out?"

I kept my eyes on the road. How much of what I'd heard could I tell Ramon? I'd been warned, threatened, and frowned at. I wasn't sure who'd meant it and who hadn't. It wouldn't be fair for me to give Ramon the wrong idea about anyone.

"I'll tell you what I know," I said. "Just give me time to get everything straight in my own mind. Okay?"

"Okay, Stacy," he said.

We turned off the highway onto a narrow dirt road that led into the forest. I parked the car just past the house where the drive ended. As we climbed from the car, Ramon gazed up at the old stone house and whistled. "It's like a castle," he said.

Glenna looked like the queen of the castle as she opened the door and waved us into the living room. In her mid-eighties, she was dressed in a dark red velvet robe and lots of gold costume jewelry. "Stacy! Hello!" she shouted and took my hands.

"Hello," I shouted back, hoping that she had turned on her hearing aid. I quickly introduced Ramon.

He stared at the nearby wall with wide eyes. Hanging there was a cow skull wearing a wreath of paper flowers.

"Sit down," Glenna ordered. "Everybody sit down."

We did as she said, and she turned to me. "How's your grandmother, Stacy?"

"Fine," I said. "Gran sent me to ask you about the mine. Now that Will Knight has died, what will happen to the land?"

"The land's paid for. Bought for cash," she said. "Would you like some tea?"

"No, thank you," I said. "When did you learn that Mr. Knight planned to reopen the silver mine?"

"Right after I signed the papers." She shook her head as she said, "That sneaky so-and-so. I know everybody's angry. Barry said they would be when I told him what Will had done. I just hope that nobody blames me. That other bid I got wasn't near enough. You understand, don't you?"

Another bid on the mine? Ramon and I glanced at each other. "Can you tell me about that other bid?" I asked.

She hopped up. "I'll get the information for you."

Glenna was gone for only a minute. When she came back she handed me an envelope. Two names and some figures were written on the back. The first bid was the Knight bid. But it wasn't Will's name on the envelope.

There was also a second bid. Across from it was the only bid close to what I guessed was the land's actual value. That bid had been offered by our chef, Eddie Jackson! Why? Eddie had made no secret of the fact that someday he wanted to open a restaurant of his own. But what would Eddie want with an abandoned mine?

I handed Ramon the envelope. "Juliana Knight, not her husband, bid for the land," I told him.

"The sale was in Juliana's name. Will said it had something to do with taxes," Glenna said. She leaned forward eagerly. "It's been a long time since Juliana's seen your uncle. As I remember, she was a pretty little thing, and Jim was crazy about her. Are there any sparks left?"

I just smiled. We thanked Glenna for her help and left.

Dark clouds were flowing over the mountains as we drove back to the hotel. I took a fistful of messages out of my box and put them in my purse. They all seemed to be from my office. I'd look at them later. It was dinnertime, and I was hungry.

Later after dinner Ramon told me, "Before I leave, I want to take one more look at the scene of the crime. I want to make sure we didn't miss something."

I went up to the fourth floor with him. But we stopped outside the door to Knight's suite. We looked at each other. We had both heard a noise coming from inside the room.

Ramon put a hand on the doorknob, and it turned. We ducked under the yellow police tape, which still stretched across the door, and entered the room. I hit the light switch.

Millie Blair nearly dropped her flashlight.

"Would you like to explain what you're doing here?" Ramon asked her.

I had a question too. "How did you unlock the door?" I asked.

She answered my question first. "I took your uncle's passkey from the hook in the broom closet where he always hangs it." She took a key from the pocket of her long, black dress and handed it to me.

I groaned. A passkey hanging in a broom closet where anyone could get it?

"You were looking for something," Ramon said. "What is it?"

Millie didn't answer so Ramon went on. "The room has been carefully searched for evidence," he said. "Whatever you're looking for has been found."

"Everything?" Millie cried out. She held onto the back of a chair for support. "I want to go home," she said.

Ramon nodded at me, so I put one arm around Millie and helped her to the lobby. When we reached the lobby, I called to Lew, one of the bellhops. Lew was going off duty, so I asked him to drive Millie home.

Ramon and I found Uncle Jim in the kitchen. He was making a cup of instant coffee. "Hi," he said. "Do you want some coffee too?"

I didn't answer. I just blurted out, "Uncle Jim, I said a lot of angry things today. But I never meant to hurt you."

He lifted his cup and took a sip. "You were right, Stacy. I thought it over. I don't make a good security chief. I decided it's time I did something I've always wanted to do." He took another sip. Then he said, "I'm going to Brazil to go fishing."

"Brazil?" I cried. "You've never wanted to go to Brazil!" All I could think about was the ticket to Brazil that Juliana had turned in. She must have told Jim she was going. But she hadn't told him yet that she'd turned in the ticket. Should I tell him? I didn't know what to say.

Ramon solved that problem. "You can't go to Brazil right now, Mr. Champagne. You're a suspect in a murder case."

"How can Uncle Jim be a suspect when we just caught Millie at the scene of the crime?" I asked. I waved the key Millie had taken. "She took your passkey, Uncle Jim. What kind of security is that? If everybody in town knows where you keep your passkey, it's a wonder we don't have all sorts of horrible crimes here!"

"Like murder," Ramon said quietly.

"Yes! Like—"

I stopped speaking, but Uncle Jim said, "If you don't like the way things are run here, then you can come back and run them yourself."

He took his coffee to his room, and I turned to Ramon. "You have to prove that my uncle is innocent."

"I can't prove that right now," Ramon said. "If you want your uncle proved innocent, then help me. You've been getting information from many people. Why can't you share it with me?"

I hesitated. Ramon said, "Okay, suppose your uncle did murder Knight. Would you want him to go through the rest of his life carrying that secret?"

Secret? I stopped worrying. Uncle Jim had never been able to keep secrets. He was too straightforward for murder and cover-ups. "I'll help you, Ramon," I said. I sat back and told him every single thing I'd learned.

Ramon nodded and put away his notebook. "That helps, Stacy. Thanks." He reached out a hand and smoothed my hair. "You look beat. You'd better turn in. I'll come by tomorrow, and we'll start digging into some of these leads you've given me."

We said good night. Tired, I stumbled into my bedroom. I tossed my purse onto the nearest chair, but I missed. The purse fell open, and its contents landed on the rug.

For the first time since I had put the messages in my purse, I saw the envelope with my name printed on it. I stared at it. It was printed in the same type that had been used on the letters to Will Knight!

I hurried to pick up the unsealed envelope. I pulled out the single sheet of paper inside. The message was simple and direct: *Stacy Champagne, do you want to be next?*

CHAPTER 9

I got very little sleep during the night. After the storm came a silence. It was so still I could hear every little noise. Every sound frightened me. Was someone trying to sneak into my room? Turn my doorknob? Scratch at my open window?

I woke at nine. I was still sleepy. But I was more sure than ever that I was going to help solve the murder. The letter writer was wrong in thinking I'd be scared off. Scared, yes. Scared off, no.

Gran and Dad were at the front desk when I went into the lobby. Gran was full of the news she had to tell me. "Morgan's back with two of his police officers," she said. "They're going over Will Knight's suite for more clues." She gave a sigh. "I'm so glad you're here, Stacy," she said. "Without your help, the police might not be able to solve this murder any more than they could solve the other one."

"What other one?" I asked.

"That was a long time ago," Dad said. "Jim was still in high school."

"It doesn't matter how long ago it was," Gran said. "No one was ever arrested for that other murder."

"Tell me what happened," I said.

Gran seemed glad to. "The historical society had its annual meeting here at the hotel. Donald Blair got here and started the meeting. Then he realized he'd forgotten to bring copies of the budget. He went back to his office in the museum to get them. That's when he discovered the fire. The fire had been set just outside the building in the alley. And while the volunteer firemen were putting out the fire, they found a body inside the museum. A man was lying on the floor near the back door. Later the police said that he had died before the fire had been set. They also thought someone had killed him in a fight, then set the museum on fire to cover up the murder."

"That's horrible!" I said.

"What's even worse," Gran said, "was that the poor man wasn't from Silver Ridge. He was a fisherman who had camped near here a number of times. He'd told the waitress in the coffee shop that he'd seen some of the kids in town smoking marijuana in the alley. But no one else had, and the man complained about an awful lot of things, so nobody really believed him."

"How did he get murdered in the museum?"

"I wish I could remember all the details," Gran said. "But I can't."

"That's all right," I said. "I'll ask Millie. She worked at the museum when she was in high school, didn't she?"

Gran gripped my shoulders. "Oh, don't ask Millie about it!" she said. "Millie's brother Jack is the one who was arrested for the murder!"

I looked at Dad. "Tell me what happened to Jack. He didn't go to prison for murdering the fisherman, did he?"

"The case never came to trial," Dad said. "Jack didn't murder anyone, and I never believed he set the fire. He was arrested because of what they found in the trunk of his car. They saw an empty gasoline container and part of a rag that matched those found in the alley."

"Jack has always been headstrong," Gran said. "He'd been angry with Donald Blair. Donald wouldn't allow Jack to take one of the exhibits to school as part of a history project. A number of people heard Jack yell at Donald that if people couldn't borrow the exhibits, then the museum was worthless. The town didn't need it." Gran hesitated. "I've always believed Jack set the fire. But I don't think he would have killed that fisherman."

"Why didn't Jack go to trial?" I asked.

"Because he came up with an alibi," Gran answered. "One of the other boys finally came forward. He said that while all their parents were attending the historical society meeting, Jack, Millie, Juliana, and he had been at the O'Connors' house playing cards."

"What other boy?" I asked. "You mean Uncle Jim?"

"No," Gran said. "It wasn't Jim. The boy who came forward was Will Knight."

I had lots of questions, but Gran was called to the phone. And Dad hurried over to help a desk clerk who was having a problem with someone's bill.

Gloria, one of the desk clerks, was free so I asked her, "Who brought a letter for me yesterday?"

"I don't know," she said. "Around four-thirty or five o'clock I found an envelope with your name on it. It was lying at the end of the desk." She smiled. "It was after you'd gone out with that good-looking deputy." She winked at me. "Tell me about him."

"There's nothing to tell," I said. "Deputy Gonzales and I are working on an investigation."

"Right," Ramon said. He stepped up behind me and asked quietly, "Are we investigating something right now?"

As we turned away from the desk, I said, "A letter and another murder."

He stopped short. "What murder?"

"Wait until I get a jacket," I said. "We'll go outside and I'll tell you about it."

I was back in the lobby in no time. The letter was in my jacket pocket. Ramon held out his hand, and I took it. I could hear fresh rumors beginning to buzz back at the front desk, but I didn't care. I led Ramon into the gardens in back of the hotel.

I began by telling him what I'd learned about the unsolved murder in the museum. When I finished I said, "There's something odd about that. Jack said he and Will had hated each other. Yet Will gave Jack an alibi. And Millie and Juliana went along with it. At the time Juliana was supposed to be dating my uncle. Were they lying? All four of them? I can't figure out why."

"One murder to solve isn't enough for you, Stacy?" Ramon asked. His eyes twinkled.

I said, "I have to solve Will Knight's murder before the murderer gets to me." From the pocket of my jacket I took out the letter and handed it to Ramon.

He frowned as he read it. "Where did this come from?" he asked.

"All I know is that it was found on the desk late in the afternoon," I said. "There's no way of knowing who brought it to the hotel."

"Yes, there is," Ramon said. "We'll find out which of our suspects was in the hotel around that time. None of them could sneak into the lobby and put the letter on the desk without having been seen by someone." He took my hand again and began to stride down the path toward the hotel. "The sooner we get the answers, the closer we'll be to catching our murderer."

This time Ramon asked the questions, and I was the one who tagged along. We ended up learning that Eddie Jackson had been in the hotel. As usual, he was in the kitchen, where dinner was being prepared. Barry Harrison had arrived around four-thirty. He had brought the week's printed menu specials to Alicia. Millie, Jack, and Tess had come to the coffee shop for the early-bird Monday night special. One of the waitresses remembered seating them exactly at five o'clock. And Juliana had been seen by a number of people as she wandered through the lobby and stood at the windows, watching it rain. Only two suspects had not been in the hotel between four-thirty and five— Officer Morgan and Uncle Jim.

"How many people know that you're helping to investigate this case?" Ramon asked me.

"Everyone in Silver Ridge. Gran didn't try to keep it secret."

"Okay, " Ramon said. "Someone might just be trying to scare you off."

"Why me? Why not you and Officer Morgan?" I asked.

"Stacy, I'm pretty sure it's because you know something we don't. Or maybe the murderer *thinks* you know something," Ramon said. "In your talks with some of the suspects yesterday, did you say anything that might point a finger at one person?"

I shook my head. Ramon said, "Then let's check out that murder that took place here in the Sixties. I'll ask for the police records. But let's start with the backdated newspapers in the newspaper office."

We walked down the hill to the print shop. I waved at Barry as we entered. "Okay if we go in the back room and look in the morgue?" I shouted over the noise of the press.

Barry nodded, so I led Ramon to a storage area, called "the morgue." It was filled with dusty boxes and file cabinets. "We came here on a field trip when I was in high school," I told him. "I think I know where everything is. We'll want boxes labeled 1964 or 1965."

I looked up suddenly. The noisy press had stopped, and Barry was standing in the doorway. "What are you looking for?" he asked. "Want some help?"

I told him, and he shook his head. "I don't keep files that long," he said. "But I've got a good memory. What do you want to know about?"

"The fire and murder in the museum," I said. "Why do you think Millie, Juliana, Will, and Jack first kept quiet about being together?"

"There was a problem about Will and Millie dating," Barry said. "After Will had been caught shoplifting, Mr. O'Connor had forbidden his kids to have anything to do with Will. I guess they were scared at being found out."

"Why was Juliana there with Jack? I thought that she'd been going with my Uncle Jim."

Barry shrugged. "They were just high school kids. It wasn't that serious. That's all I can tell you."

We thanked Barry for his help and left the print shop. Ramon said, "Next stop, police department. We can look at their records of the fire and the murder."

"Why don't you go alone?" I asked. "Morgan won't give you the records if you're with me. While you're talking to Morgan, I'll talk to Millie."

By the time I reached the museum I still wasn't sure what to say to Millie. I walked around to the alley and examined the dark-stained brick at the back door. Suddenly, the back door opened, and Millie stood in the doorway with a bag of trash. Behind her I could see Jack swinging the handle of the old printing press.

Millie looked startled. Then she turned and yelled at Jack, "Get away from there before you break something. You don't know how to run that machine."

Who did she think she was kidding? "I'm not here to talk about who uses your machine," I said. "I want to know about the man who was found dead in the museum."

For just an instant Millie's and Jack's gaze was drawn to a spot on the floor near the back door. So I learned exactly where the body had been found.

Millie didn't look me in the eye. She said, "Some people thought he set the fire on purpose so he could steal things from the museum. Then he fell and hit his head."

"On what? The corner of a table?"

"No. It was a heavy ore sample. They found blood on it."

"It doesn't make sense," I said. I turned to Jack. "What do you think happened?"

Jack glared at me. Millie turned as pale as the ghost she'd been mistaken for.

"I think what happened to that stranger," Jack said, "only shows how dangerous it is to come around the museum prying and snooping."

CHAPTER 10

At noon Ramon and I took paper-bag lunches to a rocky ledge high behind the hotel. It was quiet there with a great view of the town and the valley. While we ate, I told Ramon about Millie and Jack.

Ramon said, "Jack lied. He *does* know how to operate the museum press."

"That still doesn't tell us if Millie or Jack wrote the threatening letters." I took a bite of my apple and asked, "What did you find out from Officer Morgan?"

"Something that puzzles me," Ramon said. "Morgan is not giving this murder case his full attention. When I asked him what he has found out lately, he said he has more important things to do."

"That first murder was never solved," I said. "Maybe for some reason Morgan doesn't want to solve this one either."

Ramon frowned as he said, "A number of people in this town think of Will Knight's murderer as a local hero. Does

Morgan think he can slow the investigation so that no one is ever arrested? Like the investigation of that first murder?"

What Ramon said bothered me. "If no one is arrested, then everyone who was with Will on that last day of his life will be thought of as a possible murderer. Just like Jack is still a suspect in the museum murder."

A chipmunk crept forward. I slipped it some crumbs from what was left of my sandwich. "What did the old police records say about Jack as the prime suspect?" I asked. "The alibi from the kids who had been playing cards with Jack kept him from being charged. Everyone thought those kids wouldn't have lied to save Jack because they got into so much trouble themselves for admitting they'd been together. And I agree. What did you learn about the murder victim in the museum?"

"I saw the coroner's report," Ramon said. "Fractured skull. The blow came to the back of the head, above and to the left of the right ear."

"Could he have fallen and hit his head on that ore sample as Millie claimed?"

"It's possible."

"Then," I said, "the big question is why the fisherman was in the museum. Remember what Gran told me? That he always stopped at the coffee shop next to the museum for coffee? And that he was nosy about a lot of things? Millie thinks he came to steal valuables, but there's nothing valuable in the museum."

"I don't think the man was there to steal," Ramon said. "He was a successful businessman from Dallas. He'd have no reason to steal from a small, historical museum."

I shrugged. "So where does that leave us?"

"That leaves us investigating the wrong murder," Ramon said. "There's nothing that ties the two murders together. You're welcome to solve all the murders you like, Stacy. But I think I'll stick to this recent one."

Ramon looked at his watch. "I'm going to do a little more study on the kind of printing used on those three letters. What are your plans for this afternoon?"

"First I'm going to think more about that Sixties murder. Then I'm going to talk to Juliana," I said. "I want to know my almost aunt-in-law a little better."

I stayed on the ledge in the sunshine while Ramon made his way down the path. I didn't agree that the murder at the museum had nothing to do with the murder at the hotel. But I couldn't think of a reason they'd be tied in with each other.

While I was trying to sort out the puzzle in my mind, I saw Juliana creeping along the edge of the lawn that bordered the hotel. I remembered that she had crept exactly the same way the day that her husband had been murdered.

I watched her carefully, but when she reached the woods she was out of sight. I picked up the empty lunch bags and started down the path. I hadn't gone far, however, when I heard voices, so I ducked into the shelter of the trees and waited.

A moment later the voices drew nearer. I could hear what was being said.

"But I've already told my partner," a man said. I knew that voice. It was Eddie Jackson's.

The woman's voice belonged to Juliana. She spoke quietly, so I could only catch a few words. "But why? . . . in a hurry? . . . probate?"

From where I was hidden I saw Juliana and Eddie come around a bend in the path. Now I could hear all that they were saying.

Juliana looked upset. "But Wednesday's date is on those papers," she said. "It would look strange to everyone. That's the very day Will died."

"Listen to me, Juliana," Eddie said. "It will be in with all the other legal papers. No one will ever notice the date."

Juliana shivered. "It's colder here in the shade than I thought it would be. I want to go back inside."

"No," Eddie said. "You have to make up your mind."

But Juliana turned. She began to hurry down the path. Eddie followed. After wondering for a moment what to do, I followed too.

I caught up with Juliana before she reached the door to the lobby. Eddie was nowhere in sight. I guessed that he had gone back to his office next to the kitchen.

"Do you have a minute?" I asked Juliana. "I'd like to ask you a few questions about the night back in the Sixties when the museum was set on fire."

Juliana stopped short. Her face turned white. She began to slump forward, so I grabbed her. I helped her sit on a nearby garden bench.

She took a few deep breaths. "Leave me alone. I'm all right," she said.

"You don't look all right," I told her. "Stay here. I'll get you a glass of water."

"I don't need any water," Juliana snapped.

"Yes, you do. It will help," I said.

"Stop it, Stacy! Stop getting so involved in other people's problems!" she cried. She stumbled to her feet and smoothed down her skirt. "And don't keep trying to save your uncle from suspicion," she said. "Jim doesn't want your help. He can take care of himself. Don't interfere!"

"Interfere? I'm part of this family too," I said.

Juliana sighed as she looked at me. "I'm sorry, Stacy," she said. "I'm not saying this right or you wouldn't be so upset. Your uncle is worried because he cares about you."

I faced Juliana and said, "I know my uncle cares about me. And I'm going to keep interfering—as you put it—until this murder is solved!"

Juliana ran into the hotel. I made myself calm down, then walked into the lobby. It was time I had a talk with Uncle Jim—if I could find him.

I saw Juliana leaving the hotel with three women. I knew only one of them—Lily Chan. They were all happily talking, as good friends do. Juliana would be in good hands, but I had lost my chance to ask her any more questions.

None of the hotel staff knew where Uncle Jim had gone. My watch said two-thirty. It was late enough for the lunch rush to be over and too early to begin getting ready for dinner. I decided to talk to Eddie.

His office door stood open. I could see he was alone. "May I talk to you?" I asked.

At first, Eddie acted as if he hadn't heard me. He walked to his desk and picked up a clipboard. He wrote something on it.

"Please?" I said. "We need to talk."

Eddie sighed and looked up. "What can I do for you, Stacy?"

As I walked into his office, I came right to the point. "What's going on between you and Juliana?"

Eddie didn't answer. Instead, he strode to the office door. For a moment I was afraid he was going to walk out in anger. But he closed the door and leaned against it.

"I saw you come down the path behind the hotel," he said. "So you know Juliana and I met each other there to talk over a problem. How much of what we said did you overhear?"

"Tell me about the papers she signed."

Eddie took a deep breath. "I've always been honest with your family," he said. "I've always told them that someday I want to open a restaurant of my own."

I nodded, and Eddie went on. "I have the know-how. I just haven't had the money to open the kind of place I really want. It has to have beauty and style and really good food." He waited a moment. Then he said, "I turned forty this year, Stacy. If I'm ever going to have my own restaurant it has to be now. I went to Mrs. Sutton and told her I wanted to buy the land on the ridge where the old mine is."

"I don't get it," I said. "Who'd want to go to a restaurant on the site of an abandoned mine?"

Eddie smiled and shook his head. "Think about it. That ridge has the best view of the valley and the river and the mountains that I've ever found. I'd build a restaurant with great views on three sides. And behind the restaurant would be the mysterious old mine. Its entrance would be sealed forever."

"Oh, yes!" I said. I could see Eddie's dream in my mind.

"I'd call it *Silver House*," Eddie said. "Besides the wide windows on three sides, we'd have a round, open fireplace in the center. And we'd have banquet rooms on each side of the kitchen at the back." He stopped and looked at me. "The town needs more meeting space than your hotel can offer. You know that, Stacy."

"I know," I said. "And you want Juliana to sell it to you."

"She already did," Eddie said. "Before I went to Mrs. Sutton, I got a partner to put up the money I needed."

"Who's your partner?" I asked.

Eddie looked away. "Do you remember the man who owns the fast-food chain in Denver? The one who tried to hire me a few years ago?"

I gasped. If Eddie had been willing to go to a fast-food company for the money, he was willing to do *anything* to get his dream.

"I put in a bid, but Knight offered more than the land was worth. He got it." Eddie said. "Mrs. Sutton should have told us what Knight wanted to do with the mine."

"Don't blame her. She didn't know until after the sale. Then she told Barry. He wrote the story in *The Times*."

"See why I wouldn't have murdered Knight?" Eddie said. "I wanted to see the look on his face when he found out that his wife had come to me to sell me the land."

"Juliana came to *you?*" I asked in surprise.

"She did when she found out that he wanted to open the mine. She decided to leave Knight and needed the money. I called Vance Pickering, the lawyer. He drew up the papers, and Juliana signed them around noon on Wednesday."

"Just a few hours before her husband was murdered," I said.

"That's why Juliana wants to back out now," Eddie said. "She thinks that selling the land just before her husband died makes it look as though she murdered him."

I spoke my thoughts aloud. "Maybe that's what they were arguing about. Maybe Will Knight threatened Juliana. Maybe he used physical force. Maybe she tried to defend herself."

"Not here at the hotel," Eddie said. "Juliana could have called Security. Or she could have called me. I was in the hotel at that time."

I wasn't about to tell Eddie. But his being in the hotel at the time of the murder was one of the reasons he was a suspect.

CHAPTER 11

That evening Ramon and I sat on the hotel's veranda and watched the stars come out. The mountain peaks were black against the darkening sky. We held hands, and I hoped our talk would be about something other than murder. But Ramon said, "I found out something interesting today. Eddie Jackson closed out his checking and savings accounts the day of the murder."

"Eddie told me what he did with the money," I said. In turn I told Ramon.

I thought he'd have something to say about Eddie's plans. Instead, Ramon said, "I sent the threatening letter Knight received to a friend at the Colorado Bureau of Investigations in Denver to test. I told him that I would shovel his driveway every winter for the rest of my life if he'd rush the test results. I was thinking that since you live in Denver . . ."

67

Ramon paused, and I snuggled a little bit closer. "So every time it snows you'll be there, and . . . ?"

"Not exactly," Ramon said. "I was hoping that since you live there, you'd offer to shovel the snow for me."

The teasing in his voice was warm. I lifted my face. But just then a couple of guests from the hotel joined us on the veranda.

"It's too chilly out here," the woman said. They went back inside, but the moment was gone.

Ramon said, "About that threatening letter. It wasn't a printed letter. It was a sheet that was photocopied from the original. The letters were made up of toner. Tell me who has access to a copy machine."

"Everybody in Silver Ridge," I said. "We have one at the hotel. The drugstore has one and the post office. And you saw the copy machine in Barry's printing office. Anyone in town can use it. They just have to put a coin in the slot."

"Is there a copy machine at the museum?"

"No, but there's one in Vance Pickering's office. Eddie was there on Wednesday."

"The timing is wrong," Ramon told me. "You found the letter on Tuesday."

I let out a sigh. "Why was the letter photocopied? Why not send the original?"

"All three letters are the same," Ramon said. "They could have been copied to hide something."

"Like what?" I asked.

"I don't know yet," he said.

I shivered. It was getting much colder now that it was dark. "Let's go inside," I said.

Just inside the door Ramon gave me a light good-bye kiss on the lips. I could see the desk clerks watching, so I didn't respond the way I wanted to.

Ramon didn't understand my hesitation. "Don't worry, Stacy," he said. "You'll be safe here with your family."

I wasn't too sure about that.

Uncle Jim was waiting for me at the bottom of the stairs. "You're making a big mistake, Stacy," he said.

"You don't like Ramon?" I asked.

"Ramon's okay," Uncle Jim said. "It's what's going on I don't like. You're helping him investigate Will's murder. You're telling him all the local gossip. You're even using our own family ties to make things easy for him."

"And for us," I pointed out. "What's going to happen to you if you spend the rest of your life known as the last person seen with Will Knight before he died?"

"I can handle it. The hotel can handle it too." Uncle Jim's face was stern. "Sooner or later, people will forget about the murder. You should too."

"Forget?" I cried. "How can I forget? I shudder every time I go to the fourth floor. I haven't slept well since I found . . ." No. I couldn't tell my family about the threatening letter that was sent to me. "Just please tell me, if you can, how to forget?"

Jim reached out and hugged me, as though I were a child again. Then he put me down on the bottom stair and sat next to me. "Have you ever thought it might get to be worse if you do find out what happened to Will?" he asked.

"What are you saying?" I turned to look up into his face.

"I'm saying that there's no reason for you to investigate. Leave it up to the police. And stop trying to get information about that murder back in the Sixties. Today you really upset Juliana when you hounded her about it."

Now I knew what had upset him. He wasn't the only one. I was upset, too! "Is that what she told you? Well, that's not the way it happened."

"Calm down," Uncle Jim said. "Why do you care about that old murder anyway?"

"Somebody got away with murder. That's why I care. Don't you want to know what happened that night?"

Uncle Jim sighed loudly. "You think it's as simple as finding out the name of the murderer. But there's more to it than you know. Back off, Stacy."

"I can't," I told him.

He stood up, towering above me. "Okay, go ahead. Ask questions. Cause trouble. But don't expect my help." He turned and stomped up the stairs.

I knew that my Uncle Jim wasn't a murderer. But why was he making it so hard to find out the truth?

I stood up and slowly went upstairs. When I pushed open the door to my bedroom, I let out a yelp. Jack O'Connor was standing in front of my desk.

My room was a mess. The mattress had been pushed off the bed, and the pillows had been taken out of their cases. The dresser drawers had been emptied. Even a box of old school papers and photos had been dumped on the floor.

Jack looked scared. "I'll help you clean it up," he said.

"You bet you will!" I told him. I looked at the open window, then back to Jack. "What are you doing in my room?"

"I thought you'd be spending more time with the deputy," Jack said. "You aren't going to get to first base if you let him go home so early. You've got to show a little interest."

"My personal life is none of your business!"

"I'm trying to say that if you'd spent the evening with him, like I thought you would, I'd have cleaned all this up before you got back."

I frowned at Jack. "You're going to put everything back where it was, and you're going to tell me what you were looking for."

Jack leaned against the bedpost. "I haven't been able to sleep or think straight these last few days. I keep waiting for Morgan to come and drag me away. But I keep telling myself that they don't know yet, and maybe they won't have to find out."

I froze. Was Jack confessing to Will Knight's murder?

It was hard to breathe as I asked, "Are you looking for some evidence that shows you murdered Mr. Knight?"

"I didn't murder anybody," Jack said. "But I'm looking for a paper. Maybe it's in an envelope. You must have picked it up when you found Will."

"The threatening letter!" I said. "You wrote it!"

"I had nothing to do with that," Jack said. "Don't you know what I'm looking for?"

"No," I said. "What is it?"

"You'll know when you see it," he said. "Remember, I'm willing to pay you to get it back. I've already paid and paid for it." He took hold of the mattress and heaved it back onto the springs. "This would be easier if you gave me a hand," he said.

I helped him. Together we made the bed and put my clothes back into the dresser drawers.

Jack seemed to be talking to himself. "I wonder if what I'm looking for could still be in Will's room."

"I'm sure it isn't," I said. "Millie looked, and she didn't find anything."

Jack dropped the sweater he was folding. "What are you talking about? Will was alive when Millie was in his room."

I was surprised that Jack didn't know about Millie's search of Will's room. They were each looking for something and not telling the other.

I told Jack what Millie had done, and he said, "Millie should have shown more sense."

"Neither you nor Millie is showing any sense," I said. "Why don't you tell me what it is you're looking for?"

Jack thought a moment, then shook his head. "I can't tell you," he said. "But please, Stacy, please . . . If it turns up, promise me you'll call me right away!"

CHAPTER
12

The next morning I found Ramon sitting at our kitchen table. "Is there any chance that the officer at the scene of the crime could have found what Millie and—uh, Millie—is looking for?"

Ramon put down his coffee cup. "Are you asking if Morgan might be withholding evidence?"

"I don't know what I'm asking," I said. "But I don't think we should ignore that first murder. Why don't we drive down to Denver and talk to Donald Blair about it? He's the one who discovered the fire and found the body. Maybe there was some clue that was overlooked at the time."

"Okay," Ramon said. "I'll check in with my office while you call Mr. Blair."

I made the call, and Mr. Blair was willing to talk to us. As I waited for Ramon, I stopped at the desk to talk to Dad. He was going through some reservation slips.

"It looks as if you could use some extra help," I said.

He nodded. "I'll probably have to hire another clerk for the summer season."

"I was always a big help to you," I said. "I could help you again."

Dad looked up. "You have a good job in Denver."

"It's not that much," I told him. "If you need me—"

"We don't," he said firmly. "I expect you to make the most of your opportunities."

This rejection hurt as much as the first one. Numbly, I joined Ramon. We climbed into his car and drove to Denver.

We located Mr. Blair's address, parked, and rang his doorbell.

A tall, elderly man smiled down at me. "You must be Stacy Champagne. You were just a little girl the last time I saw you."

Ramon introduced himself and shook hands with Donald Blair, who invited us in.

Once we were seated in his living room, Mr. Blair served us coffee. We talked about Silver Ridge. Finally I asked him about the museum fire. "What do you think happened? Who do you think did it?"

"I tried to figure it out, but I never could," he said. "The museum didn't have anything valuable enough to steal."

"I was told that Jack O'Connor might have set the fire for revenge."

Mr. Blair shook his head. "Jack was a spoiled kid. Millie is worth ten of him. But Jack didn't set that fire."

"You sound very sure," Ramon said.

"I am sure. Jack and Millie have always been as close as if they were twins. Jack never would have set fire to the museum, because that would have been a tragedy to Millie."

"What about the alibi Will Knight gave Jack?" I asked.

"I never did understand why those kids were believed," Mr. Blair said. "Millie wasn't secretly dating Will. She couldn't stand him. She only went along with the story because it gave Jack an alibi. Will hadn't been playing cards with the others."

"The police report said he was," Ramon told him.

"And I say he wasn't," Mr. Blair said. "I'm the only one who saw Will alone that night on Main Street. It was while I was heading back to the museum for the budget report. I'd forgotten to bring it to the historical meeting."

"Why didn't you tell anyone?" I asked.

"I didn't think of Will until he claimed to be where I knew he wasn't. By then they'd found the gasoline can and the rag in Jack's car. I thought someone was setting Jack up for the crime and he needed the alibi. Why should I ruin it?"

I was too surprised to say anything. But Ramon asked, "Why didn't you tell that to the police at the time?"

"Hey, I'm not the one who did anything wrong," Mr. Blair said. "I'm only telling you all this now so I can help Stacy and her family."

"You're forgetting there was a murder involved," Ramon said.

"I never forgot the murder," Mr. Blair said. "But we didn't know much of anything about that fisherman fellow or why anyone would want to murder him. I'm glad they didn't put the blame on the kids."

I got to my feet. "Thanks for taking the time to talk to us," I said. Ramon and I weren't any closer to solving this first murder than we had been. All we had learned was that everyone involved in the case had been lying. And Mr. Blair—who should have known better—had deliberately withheld evidence.

Ramon dropped me off at the hotel and drove on to the sheriff's office. As I headed toward my bedroom, Gran stepped out of her room. She gave me a hug and walked into my bedroom with me. "How are you coming with the investigation?" she asked.

I sighed. "You and Ramon seem to be the only ones who want the case solved."

"Ramon is a nice young man," Gran said. She went on talking, but I didn't hear her. I could see an envelope that lay on the floor next to my bed. Printed on the envelope was my name in the same type that had been used on the other letters.

It wasn't hard to get rid of Gran. With another hug she left me, and I rushed into my room to pick up the envelope and open it.

The message came across clearly: *How often do you have to be told? Stop snooping, or you'll never make it back to Denver.*

I jumped as my door opened. It was Gran. "Did you find your letter?" she asked. "I brought it up and tossed it at the table next to your bed."

"Gran," I asked, "who brought the letter?"

"I have no idea," she said. "I found it lying on the front desk. Your box was filled with messages from your office, so I brought the letter up here." She smiled. "Open the letter and you'll know who it's from."

"Of course," I said.

"Oh! And then go see Millie," Gran told me. "I almost forgot. Millie called just before you came in. She said she needs to talk to you. She asked if you could come to the museum as soon as possible."

Ramon needed to know about this second letter. I telephoned him at the sheriff's office. I was told he had left. He'd gotten a call from someone at the museum.

I hurried as fast as I could to the museum. Millie, Jack, and Ramon looked up at me when I came in. Ramon was the only one who gave me a smile.

Millie didn't greet me. She said to Jack, "Go next door to the diner and get us some coffee."

"Decaf or regular?" Jack asked.

"Oh, who cares!" Millie snapped. "Just get something, anything, and take your time about it. In fact, go to the bakery and bring back some caramel buns too."

Jack hurried out the door. Millie pointed to some folding chairs, so Ramon and I sat with her. She leaned forward and said, "Donald telephoned me after you talked with him. He told me everything he said. So now I've got something to tell you too."

She glanced in the direction Jack had gone. "I can't keep it a secret any longer. At least I've bought all these years of freedom for him. You have to understand. Jack was so young then. It's so unfair that one childhood mistake should punish him all his life."

"What really happened?" Ramon asked.

Millie blinked. Then she sighed. "Well, as Donald told you, we didn't have a card party the night of the museum fire. And I never secretly dated Will." She sniffled, and I handed her a tissue.

"Just start at the beginning and tell us what happened," Ramon said.

Millie took a deep breath. "Mr. Blair trusted me with my own key to the museum. I always kept it on a special hook near our kitchen door, so I could pick it up on my way out of the house. I was *trustworthy*." Tears filled her eyes.

"Of course you were. You *are*," I said.

"We were all down on the street watching the fire. Will came up and pulled me aside where no one could hear us. He told me that he'd seen Jack in the alley behind the museum throwing gasoline on the building. That fisherman had heard the noise and had come to investigate. The man started yelling at Jack and said he'd call the police. They got into a fight, and the man fell. He hit his head really hard."

Millie twisted her fingers together as she spoke. "Will told me he took the man's pulse, but there wasn't one. Will and Jack talked it over and decided to drag the man's body inside the museum door. They decided the fire would cover it up. It would look as if the man had broken in, had set the fire himself, and had fallen and hit his head."

"That's close to what the police came up with," I said. "But how did Jack and Will get into the museum? Did they break the lock?"

"No!" Millie cried. "Jack had taken my key!"

She cried for a few minutes. Then she pulled herself together and said, "Will put the key into my hand himself. He said he'd taken it away from Jack. Will didn't want to be involved, so he needed an alibi too. But mostly I agreed to go along with the story to save Jack from going to prison."

"Did you talk it over with Jack?" Ramon asked. "Did he agree too?"

"Oh, no! I never said a word to Jack," Millie said. "If he thought I knew what he'd done, we always have that hanging between us. Jack's always been my best friend."

Jack came in, pushing the door open with his elbow. "Here's the coffee and caramel buns," he said. He stopped and looked at Millie. "What happened?" he asked.

"I told them the truth about the night of the fire," Millie said. "I had to tell, Jack. They already knew most of it."

Jack wrapped his arms around Millie. "It's not fair," he said to Ramon. "Millie shouldn't be punished for something she did when she was just a kid."

"What do you mean, what *I* did?" Millie cried.

"Did Will Knight have a talk with you after the fire?" I asked Jack.

Jack slumped on one of the other folding chairs. "Yes," he said. "Right after the fire, Will told me he'd been dating Millie secretly. He said that Millie used her key to open the museum at night so they could be alone. He said they used drugs too."

Millie gasped, but Jack went on. "Will said that the fisherman had seen a light in the museum. He'd threatened to go to the police. He struggled with Will. Millie was scared, so she picked up a chunk of ore and hit the guy over the head with it."

"He told you I killed the man?" Millie screeched.

"He said it was self-defense," Jack said. "But he said no jury would look at it that way because of the drugs."

"Never, never, never did I use drugs!" Millie cried. "Why did you believe that?"

I said, "Millie, you believed Will when he told you Jack killed the fisherman."

"Will told you that?" Jack jumped to his feet.

"Has Will Knight been blackmailing you?" Ramon asked.

Together they answered, "Yes. Every month."

"What were you looking for at the hotel?" I asked them.

Millie answered. "Will told me he'd written everything down and carried it with him wherever he went. If anything happened to him, it would be found."

"That was another of his lies," I told her.

Millie and Jack began arguing about mistrusting each other. I sipped my coffee and wondered about the fourth member of that make-believe card game. Why had Juliana sworn that she had been playing cards with the rest of them?

CHAPTER 13

A few minutes later Ramon and I walked toward the hotel. "What about Juliana?" I asked. "She lied about that card game too. And she didn't want us to look into the museum murder."

"It could be that she didn't want us to discover that Will had committed murder," Ramon said.

"It could also be that Juliana committed the murder herself," I said. "Does that surprise you?"

"Nothing surprises me," Ramon answered.

I pulled the second letter out of my jacket pocket. I handed it to Ramon.

He stopped in the middle of the drive. He frowned as he read the letter. "This isn't just a warning. This is a threat." He looked at me with such concern, my heart gave a couple of extra bumps. "I think you should get out of Silver Ridge, Stacy. Go back to Denver," he told me.

"I can't," I said. "I'm here to help my family."

"Then I'm going to insist that someone remain at your side night and day."

"You?" I asked. My heart began racing overtime.

"Yes, for one," he said. "Maybe Morgan's got an officer he can spare. And I'll ask your uncle to take a shift."

"Just keep the letters secret, please," I begged. "You may have to tell Uncle Jim. But I don't want anyone else to know about them—most of all my grandmother."

"All right," Ramon said. "Let's see if we can find Jim."

Instead of Jim, we came upon Gran. She twisted and grunted as she tried to push a large poster under the hood of the copy machine.

"Stay here," Ramon said to me. "I'll look for Jim."

"I'm trying to reduce the drawing of the Eiffel Tower on this poster," Gran told me. "It would look very nice on the new flyers to advertise our spring menu."

"Why don't you just take it over to the print shop?" I asked. "Let Barry do it."

"He can't get to it today, and I need the flyers before tonight."

"I'll help you," I said. Together we got the poster onto the copy machine, and Gran pushed the *reduce* button. The machine laid one copy, fourteen by eleven inches, in the tray.

I looked over her shoulder. "It didn't come out very well," I said.

Gran smiled. "No problem. All I have to do is darken the picture and letters with a pen. Then I can make my flyers from it. Watch."

After a few minutes she showed me what she had done. "Now, wait until you see this," she said. She ran off a copy on the machine and waved it at me.

It was dark and clear. "Who taught you how to do this?" I asked.

"Millie. Sometimes I let her use our machine if she's in a hurry and Barry is busy."

I thought about it. Everything went back to Barry. He had the machines. And he could use the old museum signs to provide the print. But how did he get the signs?

Gran said, "Stacy, will you please take this poster to the dining room? Then come back, and by that time I'll have a stack of flyers for you to deliver to some of the stores in town. Ask them to put them in their windows."

I had no sooner delivered the poster to *Champagne's* when Uncle Jim stepped up and took my arm. "Ramon told me you were not to be left alone," he said.

"Where is Ramon?" I asked. I yanked my arm away.

"He had some phone calls to make. He'll be along soon."

Uncle Jim walked with me back to Gran's office. I was surprised to see how upset she was. She jumped up from her desk and said to Jim, "Mary Ann from the travel agency just called. She forgot to ask if you'd like an aisle or window seat on your airline ticket to Florida."

Uncle Jim gulped, and Gran went on. "You're planning to go to Florida on Monday with Juliana, aren't you?"

"She needs me," Uncle Jim said quietly.

"She doesn't need an ex-boyfriend at her husband's funeral," Gran said.

"How do you know what Juliana needs?" Uncle Jim began.

I backed out of the office and closed the door behind me. If they were both busy, it would give me time to talk to Juliana.

Juliana opened the door of her room and invited me inside. "Please sit down," she said. She took a blouse from the chair. "I'm packing again. I suppose you know I'm going home to Florida the day after tomorrow."

"I know," I said. "Do you really want my uncle to go to Florida with you?"

Juliana sighed. "Jim is such a kind-hearted person." She smiled and said, "I haven't been able to talk him out of coming with me. He wants to help. He just doesn't understand that I have to find my own way." She walked to the window and stared out at her view of the mountains.

"Not all your memories of Silver Ridge are happy ones," I said. "There was the night of the museum fire."

Juliana turned and stared at me. "I didn't think Jim would tell you about that. I guess he had to tell you, after what happened to Will. You can't imagine what it's done to my life. I never meant to kill him."

Startled, I asked, "Your husband?"

Through her tears Juliana said, "Will told me he'd help me. He'd set the fire. He warned me not to tell anyone."

I tried to understand. "Wait a minute. It was the fisherman in the museum you murdered?"

Juliana nodded. "I went to the museum with Will. Jim had been busy with football. We'd had an argument. I thought he'd pay more attention to me if he were jealous. Oh, Stacy, we can do such foolish things and regret them so terribly later."

I hated to see such guilt in Juliana's eyes. "Will took Millie's key, and he brought some wine," Juliana said. "At the time we thought it was daring and fun. Will and I were racing through the museum, laughing and yelling. The fisherman must have heard us. He came in and grabbed my arms. I pulled away, but he came after me again. So I picked up a clay vase and hit him with it." She began to cry again. "Oh, Stacy, I killed him."

"Who started the fire?" I asked.

"I don't know. Will told me to go home, so I did. Later he came to my house. It was before my parents came home from that historical club meeting. Will told me to say we'd been playing cards with Millie and Jack. He'd already talked to them."

Something she said didn't make sense to me. I asked, "How did you hit the guy on the back of his head when he was chasing you?"

Juliana looked up in surprise. "I didn't," she said. "I just picked up the vase and swung at him. I hit his forehead. He stared at me a second. Then his eyes closed, and he fell backward."

"Against a large piece of ore?"

"Oh, no," she said. "He dropped to the floor."

"He died from a blow on the back of the head," I said.

Juliana's eyes grew wide and she stood up. "Are you telling me I *didn't* kill him?"

"I think Will was the murderer," I said.

"He told me I'd have to marry him. He kept telling me that murder cases are always left open. I could go to prison. He could turn me in at any time." She stared into my eyes. "Do you understand, Stacy? I couldn't stand the way I was being treated any longer."

"Did you murder your husband?" I asked.

Juliana didn't answer my question. Instead, she said, "Don't tell Jim. I want to be the one who tells him who murdered the fisherman. I told Jim about the blackmail. Now I want him to hear the rest."

"When did you tell Uncle Jim about the blackmail?" I asked.

"Early Wednesday afternoon," she said.

As I left Juliana, I felt sick. If Morgan learned that Juliana had given Uncle Jim a strong motive for murder, he'd be sure Jim had done it.

Gran met me back in the lobby. She handed me a stack of flyers. "Take these to all the stores in town," she said. "Be sure to give Millie some to put in the museum."

I found Ramon and showed him the flyers. "Come with me," I said. "Handing out flyers is going to be our cover."

"You watch too many old movies," he told me, but he came with me into town. "Tell me what you're trying to find out," he said.

"I'm not sure," I told him. "Please, Ramon. Just trust me."

"All right," he said. "But only because you said please."

When we reached the museum, Millie took the flyers.

"Gran made these," I told her. "Let me ask you a question. What do you do with the signs you've made when you're through with them? Do you give them to Barry?"

"Of course not," Millie said. "I just throw them out in the alley with the trash."

I began to get excited. Barry could steal the museum posters from the trash and reduce the size of the letters with his high-tech machine. Then he'd come up with a sharp, clean letter. It could be traced back to the museum type style and not his print shop.

After a few more stops to leave flyers, we went to Barry's shop. I gave him one of Gran's flyers.

He said, "I can do a better job than this."

"Yes. Sharp and clear," I said. Maybe it was the way I said it. As Barry looked at me his eyes narrowed. I wondered if he knew what I'd found out!

CHAPTER
14

We left Barry's shop. Just down the street Ramon stopped in front of a small grocery store. "I'm getting hungry," he said. "Want an orange or an apple?"

"Thanks. An apple," I said. It was then I remembered something I'd heard. At the time it didn't seem important. Now it was.

I grabbed Ramon's arm. "Gran is giving a dessert party tomorrow night at eight o'clock. I forgot to invite Millie and Jack while we were at the museum. I'll go back and ask them if you'll ask Officer Morgan and his wife. I'll meet you back at the hotel."

"It's the first I've heard of a party," Ramon said. "Am I invited too?"

"You bet!" I said. In my excitement I reached up to give him a quick kiss. "You're one of the guests of honor."

I quickly invited Millie and Jack. I asked Barry too.

They all said they would come, so I hurried back to the hotel and invited Juliana and Jim. Then I told Gran she was giving a dessert party the next evening.

"On such short notice?" Gran asked.

"You asked me to solve the murder, didn't you?"

"Have you, Stacy? Really?" she asked.

"I think so," I told her. "But I want to be sure before I say anything to Ramon or Morgan. That's why I need the party—to bring all the suspects together. They won't come if *I* give the party, but they will if *you* host it."

Gran made arrangements with Eddie to serve his famous Italian cream cake in the hotel's most comfortable meeting room. I took the stack of telephone messages from my box and began answering them. Solving the problems in my Denver office took the rest of the day and evening. I was glad. I didn't want to think about what could happen at the party.

As usual, Sunday was a very busy day. After early church services I helped with our hotel's popular champagne brunch. The last guests left around three, and everything in the dining room had to be arranged for the dinner crowd. Of course, there were early arrivals checking into the hotel, and guests still checking out. I was glad to stay busy. I didn't want Gran's party to be on my mind.

Exactly at eight Uncle Jim and Juliana came to the party. A few minutes later Jack arrived with his wife, Tess, and his sister, Millie. Right behind them were Ramon with Officer Morgan and his wife, Eleanor. Barry was the last to arrive.

As a waiter came in with champagne, Ramon said quietly to me, "Now I know what you're up to. All the suspects are here except Eddie. Where is he?"

"In the kitchen," I said. "He'll be here soon."

"This is a crazy idea," Ramon began.

Lucky for him Gran interrupted. She held her flute of champagne high. "To the success of the evening," Gran said.

Everyone sipped except Morgan. He took a long swallow and choked. His wife pounded him on the back. When he was able to speak he said, "Okay, Stacy. This has to be your idea. What's your plan?"

"I thought we could sort things out by telling the truth. No more secrets," I said. "For one thing, we know now that Will Knight was the one who murdered the fisherman in the museum."

"I don't know how you came up with that," Morgan said. "But it doesn't tell us who murdered Will Knight."

Eddie came in. He was wearing his high, starched chef's hat. He carried a beautiful Italian cream cake. The waiter cut slices and served them to each of the guests. He left the knife and what was left of the cake on the table near the door. I was glad. The cake was so good I was sure some of the guests would want seconds.

Morgan waited until Eddie was seated. Then he frowned at everyone in the room. "There was only a short time frame in which Will could have been murdered. Jim here has said all along that Will was alive when he brought the fruit basket. And the front desk called us as soon as Stacy found Will's body. We need to find out who was the last person to be with Will." Morgan stared at Uncle Jim.

"The *motive* is the most important thing," Ramon said. "Someone had a powerful reason to murder Knight."

"Everybody in this room had a reason to murder him," Morgan snapped.

"Even you," Gran said. "Will ruined your career."

Ramon spoke up. "I don't consider Officer Morgan to be a suspect."

"Well, then," I said. "Let's talk about the blackmail."

Millie gasped, and Juliana turned white. But Jack shouted, "So what if Will was blackmailing Millie and me! It isn't anybody's business but ours!"

"We were paying Will for years," Millie said. "Why would we suddenly decide to murder him?"

"Let's get back to the time of the murder," Morgan said. "You were both in the hotel at that time."

Millie glared at Juliana. "No one has said anything about Juliana. She was here too. And her room was on the fourth floor. She could have murdered her husband!"

Juliana opened her mouth to answer, but Uncle Jim spoke up first. "Juliana had already made plans to leave her husband. She didn't have any reason to murder him."

"Yes, she did," Millie said. "A wife would get *everything* if her husband died, but she wouldn't get a cent from his estate if they were divorced."

I said quietly, "Maybe Eddie would like to tell us his part in all this. He bought the mine from Juliana. Could Will have found out?"

Eddie paid no attention to the gasps of surprise. "I only wish he *had* found out," he said. "I wanted to see Will's face when he learned that he didn't own the land after all."

It was time to come to the point. "We need to talk about the threatening letters sent to Will," I said. "There were two. One letter was dated and mailed. The other was brought to the front desk."

"Stacy, do you know who wrote the letters?" Gran asked.

"Yes," I said. "The letter that was mailed was postmarked the day before *The Times* was published. *Before* the people in Silver Ridge found out that Will was going to reopen the mine. Barry is the one who knew because Glenna Sutton told him."

"Why would Barry want to murder Will?" Jack asked.

"Because Will had brought suit against Barry for libel. Barry would have lost everything—his newspaper, his job, his home in Silver Ridge. Barry went to talk to Will at the time he told us he had. But Will wouldn't listen. So Barry made a second visit. Maybe he was so angry he didn't realize what he was doing. He picked up the nearest weapon at hand—the fruit knife—and stabbed Will."

Barry frowned. "You can't prove I was the one who murdered Will. You can't even prove I'd gone to his room a second time."

"Yes, I can," I said. "Will hadn't liked the fruit on the tray that was in his room when he arrived. So Uncle Jim took it away. He brought the second tray—the one with apples in the basket—much later. It was after the others had visited Will. But you came back, Barry. You told us that you and Will shared an apple."

Barry leaped to his feet. Ramon and Morgan jumped up, too, but Barry was closer to the door. It took a few minutes for Ramon to make his way through the crush of people at the door. Then he ran after Barry.

"Barry won't get far," Morgan said. "I'll alert the boys down on the highway. They'll pick him up right away." He dialed a number on his cell phone.

Gran tried to be the perfect host. "Why don't we just sit down," she said. "Would anyone like more champagne? More cake?"

I glanced at the cake plate and shivered. The cake was still there, but the knife wasn't. Barry must have taken it.

By ten o'clock we knew that Morgan had been wrong about his men catching Barry right away. Barry was nowhere to be found. Morgan went back to the police station to begin a search. Uncle Jim and some of his ranger friends went looking in the mountains. I didn't know where Ramon had gone. I was worried about him. I couldn't sleep so I stayed in the lobby and waited for news.

I walked out on the veranda to think. The clouds had lifted. The sky was alive with stars. Barry wouldn't hide in the mountains. He wasn't an outdoors type. But the police were sure he hadn't made it to the highway. And he wasn't in his office or in his home. Where would Barry hide?

I gasped as it came to me that Barry must be safe and sound, hiding in our hotel. When he'd written the story about the Silver Ridge Hotel, he'd looked through every inch of it. He knew where to hide.

I knew too. The old fire stairs. No one ever used them. I dialed the police but I was put on hold.

Bessie, one of the desk clerks, walked over. "If you're trying to get your grandmother, she's with Mrs. Knight. Mrs. Knight kept hearing noises and wanted someone with her."

Juliana's room was next to the fire stairs!

I handed the phone to Bessie. "When the police come back on the line, tell them I think that Barry is hiding in the hotel. I'm going up the old fire stairs." I ran to the storeroom in back of the coffee shop kitchen. I opened the door that led to a set of fire stairs that were rarely used. Sure enough, there were footprints in the dust.

I climbed the stairs quietly. There was no sign of Barry on the second floor or on the third. I crept up to the fourth floor, sure I hadn't been heard. But someone stepped up to me on the landing.

Barry held up the large cake knife. "It was nice of you to come, Stacy," he said. "It saved me a lot of time in trying to get to you. I need your car keys."

"I don't have them with me," I said.

Barry moved quickly. He grabbed my wrist and said,

"We'll get them."

His eyes glittered as he slowly pushed me backward, step by step. "You did what Will only threatened to do. You took everything away from me, Stacy."

I walked backward down the stairs without trying to struggle. We reached the third floor and began walking down to the second. I wouldn't have a chance once I'd given Barry my car keys. I made up my mind what to do.

With all my strength I jerked his arm forward. Then I dropped to the stairs in a huddle. It threw Barry off balance. As he fell, I jammed my shoulders against his shins. Barry flipped over me. He rolled and bounced down the rest of the stairway. He lay without moving, his neck bent in a strange way. I could see that Barry was beyond help.

I heard a voice below. Feet pounded up the stairs.

"Ramon!" I called. "Ramon, I'm up here!"

Ramon ran up the stairs to the landing. He paused where Barry lay. It took only a moment before he was beside me. "Stacy!" he cried out and took me in his arms. "Did he hurt you?"

I shook my head. If I tried to speak, I would cry.

Ramon helped me up and led me through the door to the third-floor hallway. Dad was standing there with Gran.

I was still shaking. I couldn't talk. So Ramon told them what had happened.

Gran threw her arms around me. "Stacy, please don't go back to Denver," she said. "We need you here in Silver Ridge. You'd be a much better Chief of Security than Jimmy has been."

Even after all I'd been through, I was shocked. "Gran! You wouldn't fire Uncle Jim!"

"Of course not," she said. "I'll promote him to Manager of Outdoor Events. He could be in charge of fishing contests, hikes in the woods, and cross-country ski races."

My father put a hand on my shoulder. "We do need you, Stacy," he said.

"You mean it?" I asked. "You really want me to stay?"

"Of course we do," Dad said. "I've never been good at putting my feelings into words. But I've always been proud of you. I'd always hoped that someday you'd want to work at the hotel. But I had to let you know you were free to go wherever you wanted."

Dad was Dad, and there was no changing him. But he'd said he wanted me to come back. And he meant it. I smiled. "I'll take your job offer," I said.

Ramon grinned. "That was easy," he told me. "I thought I'd have to talk you into it."

Chief of Security, I thought. A fine-sounding title. But what would it cover? I'd begun my job by solving a murder. What could possibly be next?